FAMILY
HOLIDAY

FAMILY HOLIDAY

Patricia Burstein

William Morrow and Company, Inc.
New York   *1982*

Library of Congress Cataloging in Publication Data

Burstein, Patricia.
  Family holiday.

  I. Title.
PS3552.U7655F3   813′.54   81-16865
ISBN 0-688-03752-6   AACR2

Printed in the United States of America

First Edition

1 2 3 4 5 6 7 8 9 10

BOOK DESIGN BY MICHAEL MAUCERI

*For my father, who bailed me out, always,
with his love and demand for excellence;
and my mother, who softened the effect of
his commands with her gentle insight*

Acknowledgments

To my sisters, Jessica, Ellen and Karen, and brothers, John and Judd, for their devotion; Flo Kennedy for her wisdom; friends Judy Kessler, Eleanor Swertlow, Patrick Meehan, Sr., Paul Carey, Betty Spiegel, Mary Vespa and Martha Smilgis; assistant editor Naomi Cutner for her caring and helpful suggestions; copy editor Betsy Cenedella for her sharp fixes; Elizabeth and James for looking after me; and with deepest love for Nanny and Devin; and kudos to my agent, Freya Manston, and editor, Pat Golbitz.

1

"*I am enveloped by the emblems of your love, intimate reminders of the only gentleness I have known in my life. I awaken in your 'sleep, sleep, sleep' sheets, wrap myself with the robe you brought me from India, shower with your Aramis soap and put on the beige dress we bought together in Palm Springs. It is all quite unintentional. Yet these objects draw me to them. I reach out and you are not here. It is not your fault. Nor mine, perhaps. I tried to love you, but could not dislodge my father from my psyche. All the pains from my childhood intruded on our love. It was you who awakened a dead part of me, and now I fear that I shall smother it, shut the door on all those deep feelings. It's cold inside this apartment on this static Sunday. Always I could count on you, the British Thermal Unit, to keep me warm, more reliably than the landlord's heating policies in this luxury building. Now the fresh snowflakes are turning the bare tree branches in Central Park into wisteria, as I lie here, thinking of you."*

She put down her diary and crawled back under the covers wanting to be alone in bed with her fantasies. It was noon on her white digital clock radio. If Leslie got up now she could ward off that stale, wasted feeling from rising late in the afternoon. In recent times she often stayed in bed a good part of the weekend. Her sleep was fitful, with periods of waking that only served to remind her that she wanted to blot out the day. She pulled a blanket over her head to restore the darkness.

The phone rang just as she thought to take it off the hook.

"Hello, Leslie."

"Oh, hello, Mom." Her voice was husky with sleep.

"Did I wake you?"

"No." She squinted at the sunlight bouncing off the white venetian blinds.

"Leslie, if you want to come to Anlucia, let me know. I have to let them know by Friday. I'm holding your plane reservation, and they're keeping your room."

There was an edge of nervousness to her voice which might be attributable to her customary eagerness to have her children close and her anxiety about rejection. But it might be just her favorite habit of worrying, in this instance about getting to the airport on time two weeks hence. Sickness was also high on her list of provocations for worry It was her only occasion for demonstrativeness—which took the form of feeling a hot, clammy forehead. And she had shown a cool efficiency in cleaning up puddles of vomit during an outbreak of stomach virus when the children were little.

"And I'd like to know how you are."

"Fine."

"I haven't seen you in a month. When are you coming home?"

Leslie wanted to insist she *was* home, in her apartment. But that would only hurt her mother, and she saw no reason to push the point. The fact that the thought even crossed her mind betrayed some uncertainty, some confusion on her part.

"Rebecca is coming home later," her mother suddenly announced. "She's been in bed with the flu."

"Then why doesn't she stay there?"

"She says she's not getting any better because the germs can't get out of the apartment."

"*What?*"

"I don't know . . . that's what she says."

"*That* doesn't make any sense, Mom."

Leslie paused to consider her younger sister's wayward germs. How could her mother, an educated professional, bow to such illogic? At the same time, Leslie was deeply moved by those maternal feelings that overshadowed any reason.

"Okay, Leslie," she sighed. "I'll wait to hear from you."

"Oh, if you see any of Rebecca's germs in the upstairs hallway, be sure to remand them to her room."

Her mother chuckled. While she appreciated a joke, she was too shy ever to tell one.

"Bye, Mom."

Leslie hung up the phone and fumbled for a cigarette. Smoking was fast becoming her major hobby. She could do it by herself.

Christmas was two weeks off, and she wondered if she would go to Anlucia. She was lonely during the holidays only when she considered that people were supposed to be with their families, to hold down the suicide statistic. She had always gone, for as many years as she could remember, and she asked herself if she had the strength to say no.

Leslie remembered the three rows of presents filling the library of the English Tudor mansion. Bikes, Victrolas, ice skates, records, ski sweaters, cinch belts and checkers, all buffers against the poverty her father had known as a child. By the time she was fifteen, this Christmas celebration gave way to Caribbean vacations. "I'll send you down to Anlucia," her father would announce, as though wrapping a package for shipping.

Her mother would march all the children through the airport, and the check-in clerk would marvel at how this "widow" orchestrated the travel arrangements. Her father, a workaholic, would appear magically on the island at some point and stay a day or two. He was in excellent shape from running all his life from airport to airport on international legal matters. His appointment the previous year to the federal court bench had not changed anything. He labored long into the night over decisions which he wrote himself rather than delegate them to a law clerk, fresh out of Yale Law and hired for that function. His arrival on holiday was usually preceded by calls saying he could or could not get away. Her mother would nervously shuttle between the dinner table and the hotel conference room. "Oh, it's my husband," she would assure herself when summoned to the phone. After five days of long-distance conversations she had drummed up enough drama to engage other guests in the guessing game. He would arrive, briefcase in hand, after an all-night flight.

The children would scramble off the beach and squeal, "Daddy." Each would get a pat on the head and a kiss. Her mother would then lead him along a concrete walkway to their beach-front cottage. Barrel-chested men in matching seersucker trunks and jackets would nod sheepishly and say, "I see your husband has arrived." She would smile victoriously. Two days later he would vanish to his suite of offices in the cold city.

But now that the children were grown and no longer living at home her father would stay on holiday for as long as five days at a stretch, like someone trying to catch the last flicker of sunlight. Still, he was the only person Leslie knew who could feel marooned in a hundred-dollar-a-day resort. He sat up in a chair and underlined legal documents with a pencil. Occasionally he took a break to beat her younger brother in a swim to the raft.

Leslie climbed out of bed and stumbled into the bathroom. Her towels were neatly draped over a rack. Only her cleaning woman, Odessa, a quiet drinker, could have arranged three different sets in a kaleidoscope of colors. Leslie thought about locking up the liquor, but instantly rejected the role of suburban housewife. Her wallpaper, a collage of her by-lined articles from Buenos Aires to the Bahamas to New York, was intact. It was a practical solution to guests who liked to read in the bathroom and left her magazines soggy. She showered and brushed her teeth, squeezing the toothpaste out of a mangled tube. Intending to stay home and read the Sunday paper, she threw on an old pair of corduroy pants and a shirt with a hole in the elbow.

Moving now into the living room, she appreciated the symmetry of the white Haitian cotton sofa and matching chairs, arranged around a mahogany coffee table that reflected a beige shag rug in its chrome base. Her Bloomingdale's showroom was enlarged by a panoramic view of the park and a column of Fifth Avenue buildings resembling cutout figures. Outside, boys with hockey sticks scurried across the ice-smooth reservoir. She heard the clippety-clopping of hansom cab horses four floors below on the street. The clean light of midday put a shiny finish on framed pictures of Leslie with various celebrities whom she had profiled for her magazine. Her favorite was a lunging handshake for Golda Meir. She recalled how the late Israeli president had figured her for a sabra and tried to enlist her in the army. Leslie's trademark was a Jewish Afro—an Isro. She liked it to grow wild as a symbol of the mumblejumble under her scalp. But the casual observer took note instead of alert hazel eyes and perfectly tailored tweed suits.

Three plants on the windowsill appeared tired and bent. If Leslie could not revive them she would leave them in the incinerator room where, she hoped, some building attendant would rescue them. Leslie turned on the stereo and filled the apartment with Mozart horn concerti. As a child she had grown up with Beethoven thundering through the big old house on Sundays, pounding on her door, a breakfast bell summoning everyone to the table, with freshly made pancakes stacked high on plates. With Leslie at the piano and Rebecca and Jason playing cello and violin, the children gave their father Haydn trios instead of Bermuda shorts for his birthday. The heavy black 78 rpm recordings he made of these concerts sat in a storage box somewhere.

She was thirsty and stepped into a white kitchen decorated with utensils tacked to the walls. The oven mittens and carving knives got as much use as the tiny lemon soap balls that decorators put in the bathrooms of neocolonial homes. Leslie opened the empty refrigerator and looked at her life. There was one carton of orange juice, and she poured a glass.

A staccato buzzing went off in the apartment. She hoped it had nothing to do with the stove—merely a place to put pots and pans that did not fit in the cupboards. The noise got louder and more insistent, like a pneumatic drill. Tracing it to the intercom in the hallway off the bedroom, she snatched the earphone to stop this assault and nearly ripped the wire cord out of its socket.

"Miss Rittman, there's a gentleman here to see you."

"I'm not expecting anyone," she said. "Could you ask who it is, please?"

"Hold on a minute." There was the muffled sound of Mike's hand over the phone. He hadn't gotten promoted from doorman to concierge by mishandling people. Awed by the white-maned powerbroker staring at him across the desk, Mike stiffened in his cardboard-gray uniform and assumed a poker face. More fumbling and then, "Wait, I'll put him on." Then Mike busied himself with mail left from the day before.

"Hello . . . hello." Now Leslie was curious about the identity of this Sunday intruder.

"Leslie, I was just passing by your building and thought I'd see if you were in."

She recognized the Irish brogue and wished he were as faithful to his wife as to the native tongue. There was a hint of trepidation in his voice, leaving her amused by the contradiction of his bravery on the compaign trail, in some of New York's toughest districts, and his uneasiness on her turf.

"I'm sorry, but I'm really quite busy."

"It'll just be a minute."

"Unfortunately, that's just not possible."

"Did you have breakfast?"

"Yes," she snapped at him. Leslie did not like the liberty he took with her, showing up at the building unannounced, and felt justified in lying. In the past she had admired his liberal politics and had told him so over cocktails one evening after a fundraiser she covered for her magazine.

But closer scrutiny revealed that he practiced the same hackery as any backroom wheeler-dealer. The same evening no check had been brought to the table by their overly solicitous waiter. And John had seemed more focused on her bronzed body than on those children with exposed bones on posters warring against poverty, a favorite cause of his. Like many Irishmen who had grown up in deprived neighborhoods and worked their way through the wards, John was saddled with a pale, flat-chested, parochial-school graduate who could pass for a gym teacher or a waitress in a diner. As a consequence he was hopelessly attracted to dark-skinned, driving women with ample breasts and suntanned tennis legs. Though able to seduce the voters, John was, in her opinion, the Harold Stassen of romance. He was forever calling her with alleged news tips and then inviting her out, only to be turned down. Leslie was revolted by his musky older-man aroma and allergic to his pinky ring.

"Is Brahms playing?" John strained to hold on to the conversation.

"No . . . Mozart," she said, contempt now rising in her tight voice. Leslie pumped on the heels of her bare feet and did deep knee bends to crescendo notes. She admired her feet, starchy clean, as though she had emerged from a swimming pool, and free of any corns or bumps. She was convinced that soft hands and feet were the legacies of a pampered background.

"I guess I'll be on my way," John offered tentatively.

Leslie said nothing, the silence as baffling as the faraway ocean in a conch shell. She twirled the tiny black earphone, dangling from its cord, in the palm of her hand, then put it back on its slender hook.

The intrusion seemed all the more cruel at a time when Leslie was inclined to give herself over to false starts, imagining Adam at her door: jabbing his finger on the buzzer, braving one more touch of a hot stove, though forewarned by experience, still fanned by his love for Leslie. But in the end Adam knew better than to stay, though unable to form any words, heartbreak splintering his voice. He packed hurriedly, the sound of the broad leather straps as he buckled his suitcase whiplashing Leslie, the clamping of the last two snaps, cold and unforgiving in its finality, halting her desperation. Then he walked out and caught the late flight to San Francisco. Adam had gathered up everything, had left nothing behind, not even a stray sock or handkerchief caught in the fold of a nightgown or towel. He had been gone three weeks. It felt like yesterday, and forever.

Opening the door, Leslie lifted the Sunday *New York Times* off the carpeted hallway floor, immediately discarding the advertising inserts and sales coupons that dropped out of the paper as she unfolded it. She hated to shop, but knew several women who received get-well cards from Bonwit's if they failed to show by ten in the morning. Leslie was also bored by the price fluctuations of round roasts and chuck steaks. However, she kept tabs on the weather and followed the obituary page closely to avoid the shock of a phone call.

She could not concentrate. A force was building in her, and she tried to hold it back by shoving one hand in her crotch and squeezing both legs together. With the other hand she turned the pages of the paper, but the words receded before her eyes. Now she unzipped her pants and dug both hands inside, tickling a thicket of dark pubic hair and massaging her clitoris with her free hand. But the urge could not be so easily dismissed. Leslie got up from the sofa and went into the bedroom, where she pulled off her clothes and laid them at the foot of the bed. Then she opened her dresser and reached for her vibrator, buried under a mound of nightgowns. She plugged it into an extension cord on the floor, flicked the switch, then looked at Adam's soft full mouth and witty eyes in the photograph next to her. She guided the vibrator over her venus hump, but missed by a fraction of a second. The gadget got hot quickly, and she waited for it to cool. A friend had warned that it would lead to nothing short of electrocution. DEAD FROM MASTURBATING . . . she could see the headlines. Leslie turned on the vibrator again, placed it on the exact spot, sore with desire, and let it go. Her heart was pounding, and she lay like a stricken animal. Reaching down, she felt a hot sticky liquid inside her upper thighs. Her whole body, wet and warm, quaked with small tremors, and suddenly water rushed out of her eyes, like a pipe that had burst. . . . Leslie pressed her face in the soft dry pillow and wrapped herself in her own arms.

Darkness was starting to blacken the pastel skies of twilight when she woke. She unraveled her sleepy body and got up to drag the paper into the bedroom. She turned on a reading light overhead and plowed quickly through articles on political turmoil and corporate take-overs then impatiently pulled out the travel section, which she ordinarily saved for last, bracing herself for the asterisks and fine print of the bargain vacation specials.

After poring over the paper for a while, she felt the need for fresh air and decided to go for a walk. She stacked the newspaper neatly on the bottom shelf of the bookcase and went into the bathroom to wash her smudged fingers. The eerie blue computerlike lights of her stereo flashed in the living room, and she shut it off.

As she left the building the doorman said, "Good evening," and shivered as a warning against the cold. The wind was merciless as she turned the corner to Sixth Avenue. At the deli she paid for a ham sandwich, a tomato, and a carton of milk with a forty-dollar check and pocketed the change. Then she walked next door, to a stationery and cigar shop managed by an Israeli woman and the German shepherd she had bought a year before after four burglaries. The dog had grown into a wolf and Leslie did not trust Eva to restrain him. The woman's English was unintelligible and Leslie was sure that the dog could not understand Hebrew. Though she had grown up with three dogs, two cats, turtles, parakeets and chameleons, Leslie was uneasy around strange animals. If she saw a sign on the highway saying "zoo" she swerved into another lane.

She tapped on the window to catch Eva's eye, then shot ten fingers out twice. Eva opened the door slightly and slipped twenty lottery tickets through the crack, in exchange for a twenty-dollar bill. Leslie stashed them in her sheepskin coat and walked home.

Inside the lobby there was a pink message slip which she stuffed in the other pocket. She called Lara back.

"Hi."

"Nicole and I are going to grab a bite and see a movie," Lara said. "Then we might stop by Howard's party if it's still going on. Do you want to join us?"

"I'd like to, but I have to catch up on some work."

"Are you sure?"

"Positive. Thanks anyway."

Leslie hated to be evasive with such a good friend, but did not want to put a pall on her evening. Her diary lay on the night table. It was open and she picked it up.

"The day passed."

She went into the kitchen and sliced a tomato. With a quarter, she frantically peeled the lottery tickets, never pausing long enough to clear each line fully. Her head was heavy, racing over the tickets. She came up a two-dollar winner. No escaping to Bora-Bora this year, she thought. Taking the sandwich out of the bag she put the eighteen losing tickets inside, tiny gray scrapings still stuck to their edges, and dropped them in the wastebasket. She unwrapped the sandwich, sliding it onto a plate along with the tomato. Then, standing over the Formica top next to the sink, Leslie ate dinner alone.

She undressed while running the tub water, then stood on her toes to peek at her body in the medicine chest mirror. Her belly was flat and this pleased her. She caught a glimpse of her thighs, firm from a lifetime of sports. Though obsessed with staying fit, she did not keep a scale in the apartment, and the only full-length mirror, inside the bedroom closet, had been left by a former tenant. What little makeup she wore, some lipstick and blush-on to flush her cheeks, Leslie applied in the medicine chest mirror. It had never occurred to her to own a vanity table. As it was, if she stared too hard in the mirror a foreign expression would appear and frighten her. She remembered lying on the bed as a child and trying to figure out the mysteries of creation, touching herself everywhere to make sure she existed.

After a hot bath Leslie pulled a nightgown off the shelf and got into bed. Except for doormen blowing whistles for cabs to take people to restaurants and parties, the city was quiet on Sunday nights. So she did not reproach herself for the stack of unopened invitations on the table. For the moment she had a reprieve from worry about not using the fur coat her mother had bought her—one for Leslie, one for Rebecca, like the new fall coats of childhood. She watched the seven o'clock news and then read for a half hour. As she put out the track lights overhead the phone rang. It was her father, who was just leaving his chambers after a weekend of reviewing and writing motions.

"This is Daddy," he said. "Did Mommy call you about Anlucia?"

"Yes."

"Are you coming?"

"I'm not sure."

"That's ridiculous. You have time off. You come with us," he ordered.

"I think I may have something on then." It was a tepid answer, all she could manage.

"Well, let Mommy know," he said, trying to soften the command. "How is everything?"

"Fine."

It would be easier to go than not to. Alone in her bed she thought about the sun, a veteran lover, and saw herself running into the sea just as the waves pulled back, a flirtation with childhood, receding fast.

2

In the early morning hours the lobby was usually deserted, except for the nightman on the crushed velvet sofa rubbing sleep out of his eyes. But that Saturday the walnut-paneled elevator opened to the glare of klieg lights and a tangle of wire, cameras and crew. A young man in blue jeans and a turtleneck sweater that framed an unshaven face startled Leslie as she walked out of the elevator.

"Stay back," he whispered, putting his index finger to his mouth to command silence. "We're making a movie."

"I have to catch a plane," she protested.

"I don't care what you have to catch," he shot back with ferocious self-importance.

Armed with a sturdy suitcase and three wood tennis rackets, she defied his order and marched through the movie and out the front door. The nightman, whose gargantuan body had once deflected the bullet of a would-be robber, cleared the way. Outside, he stood with one foot on the curb and the other in the street and hailed a cab. She folded two dollar bills into his hand while the driver tossed the suitcase upright on the floor next to him. Before he could slam the door, Leslie rearranged the bag, making sure that the metal handle of his meter did not puncture it.

"Where to?"

"Kennedy . . . Biwi." Leslie liked the sweet, almost childlike, sound of the abbreviation for British West Indian Airways.

"What time is your flight?"

"Seven-thirty."

"We'll get you there."

Crossing Park Avenue, Leslie felt she was in the clear. Rows of miniature Christmas trees were beginning to wilt, taking on a sickly green hue. The city was still, its life turned inward, to family and home, the refuge from Salvation Army supplicants, late office-party revelers and wall-to-wall shoppers—unwanted commotion, but company of sorts for Leslie. Christmas Day was finally upon her, the dread of it, at least, over for this year. At this moment in her life, she had no place to go here and was relieved to be getting out of town.

The taxi climbed the Fifty-ninth Street bridge, with the city looming to the right, then quickly blurring out of view. Now the car sped along the highway, its dividers a murky brown from the melting snow. The slush from her shoes had become a gray puddle on the floor of the cab. Leslie leaned forward to look at her sallow complexion in the rearview mirror. It was a time for renewal, and in four hours the sun would distract, warm, comfort and eventually cast a patina over her gloom.

"Where you headed?" The driver yawned as he spoke and shook his thick black hair into place.

"Anlucia."

"You'll be nice and brown," he said cheerfully. He

looked to be about her age, early thirties, with dark good looks and sardonic lines around the mouth. But there was a blue vinyl aura about him and his brand-new taxicab.

"How long have you been driving a cab?"

"I own three and have two young kids driving for me," he said in a matter-of-fact tone. "I just came out this morning because I couldn't sleep, and I figure I'll quit in a few hours."

"So you're in business for yourself," she said kindly.

"Yeah. What do you do?"

"I write for *You* magazine."

"Do you like it?"

She was relieved that he did not say that she must meet a lot of interesting people in her line of work. "It's okay," she said wearily. "I interview a lot of celebrities."

"So?" he inquired softly.

"So, they should be interviewing me."

"You're probably right," he chuckled. "But if the interview is anything like the trivial questions I get in my cab, it's no fun. It's just lucky I don't have to answer to anyone."

One day, Leslie thought with begrudging admiration, she too would be able to banish the word *boss* from her own vocabulary. Though relentless and aggressive in her own reporting, fear ruled her in the office. Wound up in recent times by the resident feminist-coquette, who opened her mouth and legs for advancement, Leslie marched like a marionette toward the chief editor's office to make a protest. But his tightly shut door snapped the string that propelled her and she fled, too ashamed to ask for a raise despite having brought two exclusive interviews that month to the magazine. In her frustration Leslie made a few long-distance calls on the company and chalked up imaginary lunches on her expense account. Daddy was inaccessible, so she would take what she could. As a child she had gotten her father's attention by not bringing back change from the dollar he gave her for a quarter ice-cream cone.

The taxi nosed its way into a lane leading directly into Kennedy Airport. In the distance a 747 inched sleepily toward its berth between two planes stretched out on the tarmac. The cab then swung up the terminal ramp and stopped at the top, where a limousine with a license plate bearing her father's initials purred at the curb. Her mother had put Clarence, the chauffeur, on standby until the flight left.

For over thirty years Clarence had stood by the family, remaining fiercely loyal and protective. Though he sometimes cracked that he graduated from "the school of hard knocks," Clarence was no collector of injustices. Time had not put any hard lines into his black face with its big almond eyes. At sixty-seven he had the stamina of a man half his age. There was nothing that Clarence could not fix or grow, and the flowers blooming all over the Rittmans' grounds were testimony to this. If anything were to happen to this seemingly indestructible man, her mother said repeatedly, she would have to close up the house. Leslie's father, who labeled most people lazy if they left their offices before midnight, often scolded Clarence for working such long hours.

When Leslie was a little girl, Clarence had been a father figure to her. During her parents' parties, Leslie called to him from the second-floor staircase, begging him to come up to her room. He obliged with piggyback rides, hugs and kisses, and then tucked her into bed. The other children tumbled in and out of his arms like circus performers. The daughters were convinced that Clarence was possibly the handsomest man who had ever lived. Later he would feel the sting of their rejection, when as teenagers they warded off his affectionate play, even going so far as to complain to their father about his being too frisky. Clarence then busied himself with their younger brother, helping him build a poolroom in the basement, all the while grieving about the daughters' growing up. But his disappointments never became resentments, only sadnesses.

Clarence liked to wait at the airport, a connection to his own Caribbean holiday, now part of his annual bonus. He sent everyone postcards of the sunset and brought back key cases and wallets with tiny maps of the islands stitched into them. At home he kept beach posters next to a collection of Nancy Drew mysteries he found in the attic. After his divorce Clarence had moved into an apartment he renovated above the garage, once a stable, that was set back from the main house. Leslie's father, who refused all divorce cases on the grounds that he disliked "yenta talk" and did not want to act as "some crazy woman's psychiatrist, lover or surrogate father," handled the matrimonial problem. He did it for free, on the one condition that Clarence not engage him in legalisms while ferrying him to and from the office.

A porter pushed the baggage cart in the direction of the cab. Leslie waved him away, grabbed her suitcase, and rushed through the automatic door that opened in her path. Inside, her mother alternately flipped through a stack of tickets and kept watch for late arrivals. None of the children liked to rise early, and the girls had even been late for their brother's Bar Mitzvah. The rabbi had reproached them with a sermon about the insouciant attitude of assimilated and overly educated Jews. Her mother fretted more about their being on time for a flight than for such an occasion. Jason's passage into manhood could be delayed, even subverted, but the plane would not wait.

"Oh, Leslie," she exulted, the tight look of concern on her face broadening into a warm smile. "You're here. Good."

"Hi, Mom. Where's everyone?"

"They went to buy some books and magazines," she

said, opening her pocketbook to pull out a few bills. "Here, get something for yourself."

"I have my own money," Leslie said, gently pushing aside her mother's hand.

"Don't be ridiculous," her mother retorted, shoving the money into the pocket of Leslie's raincoat. "Your father gave me something for each of you. Take it."

The ticket counter, staffed by clerks who worked at a calypso pace, was utter bedlam. Passengers with tennis rackets tucked under their arms sweated in line as though they had just played rugged matches. Flurries of tickets, like so much confetti, were waved overhead in vain attempts to get official attention. Away from the crowd, a black supervisor stood silently, except for the bleeping sound of his two-way radio, listening politely to Mrs. Rittman's spiel about how the family had flown on BWIA for years. Promptly, he ushered them into the VIP lounge, where the hostess brought them orange juice, warm croissants, coffee and, later, their baggage tickets.

"How come you didn't tell him you go to Sardinia every August?" Leslie teased, referring to her mother's annual stay on the Italian island. As a poor newlywed, she had not had the requisite number of pennies to get into a canasta game in her Brooklyn apartment house. Now she was a card-carrying international traveler and she let everyone know it.

Her own children's lives were not marked by such dramatic passages. Here they sat, two of them in their twenties, and Leslie thirty, waiting to be delivered, as a matter of course, to Anlucia for the fifteenth Christmas in a row. Time froze on holiday and they held it back, just as it seemed to hold them.

"You look good, Leslie," her younger sister offered.

"I do?"

"Yes, I really like your haircut."

"Really?" Two days before, a hairstylist had snipped at her last cut, explaining how he had to undo the whole thing. He then mowed her curls into a flattop.

"It looks cute," Rebecca persisted.

"It's not too short?"

"No." She sighed. "I don't like it when it's too long."

Criticisms were indisputable facts for Leslie, compliments forever riddles.

Rebecca, with her slim body and golden cinnamon hair was Leslie's missing part. As a child, Leslie fantasized sneaking into her baby sister's room in the middle of the night, chopping off her Indian braids and taping them to her own head. (Nowadays they sent people to Bellevue for surgical reattachment of veins and nerves as fine as a hair.) Leslie had wept over the tight curls that made her ashamed to go to Sweet Sixteen parties. Now anyone who wanted to be with Leslie had to know that her hair came with her. Adam liked to pick out the curls and addressed her affectionately as "Tennis Ball Head," further endearing himself to Leslie. People always looked twice when Rebecca entered a room, but she longed to be known for her superb graphics. Leslie's professionalism, which she wore like a shawl over her sensual body, inspired neuter greetings like, "Oh, *You* magazine is here." The two sisters often went to parties together, Leslie promoting Rebecca's drawings while Rebecca arranged Leslie's shoulder strap or rubbed a smudge of blush-on into her face.

In a circle of chairs away from everyone else in the VIP lounge, their brother, Jason, buried himself in a book. His dark, seraphic curls were shorn in deference to the Wall Street firm of Pickett & Finch where he worked as an investment analyst. "I'm not your typical Yiddishe boy," he joked about the firm, "but this place may be a bit much." Unfortunately, his barber had overlooked a cluster of locks, crowning his head like a yarmulke. Relentlessly preppy,

Jason wore Weejuns from Brooks Brothers and horn-rimmed glasses on the bridge of his nose, which was not quite large or hooked enough to be called Jewish, but what the partners at P&F might describe as "interesting, in a Semitic sort of way."

At Jason's side was his wife, Holly, who sat well with the firm at their quarterly gatherings for spouses at a partner's Park Avenue co-op. She was wearing one of her WASPish Annie Hall outfits, the broad quilted skirt with uneven hemline, clashing pink vest, a blouse of unpressed cotton material, and knee socks. The effect was one of both studied indifference and absent-mindedness, neither of which was true of her. Tall, trim and flat-chested, she moved gracefully. Four months pregnant, she showed only a hint of a belly. She had recently left her job as a publicist to devote full time to impending motherhood. The two of them decided that if the baby was a boy he would not be circumcised. The Pentagon Papers paled next to The Circumcision Papers, a volley of letters between Jason and his father with copies sent to all family members.

Resentment swelled inside Leslie at the sight of her sister-in-law on the family holiday. It was not so much her presence as the remembrance that three years before, when Holly was just Jason's girl friend, Leslie had not been told that she would join them for the first time. Tentative about the trip, Leslie had packed everything she would need into a small suitcase, the precise weight she could manage. The fact of Holly at the airport was like extra luggage thrust into her arms, a duffel bag full of unknown contents that threw Leslie further off balance.

Or was it that her parents' ready acceptance of Holly was an annoying reminder of their meddling in Leslie's life? Boyfriends were not permitted to stay overnight, not even in a guest room, in case they might leave stains on the sheets. Were Jason's secretions holier than Adam's?

Maybe the answer to her parents' attitude toward Holly was the fact that she was not their child. Leslie remembered the time Rebecca had lain on a hospital stretcher with intravenous needles in her arm and tubes up her nose, antibiotics pumping into her system, which was severely infected from an IUD. "Don't tell Daddy what's wrong," she begged Leslie, who was on the lookout for their father's arrival at the emergency room. "He doesn't like it if I put anything foreign into my body." Perhaps it was just a simple matter of her parents not caring a whit about Holly or her sexual activity. For Leslie, such indifference could only be a blessing.

"Would one of you please go outside and find out when the plane is leaving?" her mother asked, looking up from her newspaper. "I have to call your father." After wrapping up some motions for impending trials, he would join the family in a day or two.

"Jason," the sisters said in unison.

"Why me?" he wailed, mortification giving his chubby cheeks an instant sunburn.

"Because you're the youngest," Rebecca threatened. "Don't be so damn lazy."

His eyeglasses bumped indignantly on his nose. "If you're both so grown up," Jason argued, "then why are you still going on vacations with Mommy and Daddy?"

Holly, who usually shrank from such disputes so as not to compound them, sat at the edge of her seat, awaiting an answer.

"Oh, please," Leslie shot back, more at her sister-in-law than at Jason, "you're the Big Married Man."

Jason put his analytical training to good use at all times. But logic could not untangle his predicament as the baby in the family. On holiday they had paraded him around like a musical comedy star, billing him as "the forty-year-old midget." A straw hat was pulled sideways over his forehead to make him look like Maurice Chevalier on an old album jacket. At ten, he had already been insufferably officious.

Now, though, he was given a momentary reprieve. "Flight Forty-six is now boarding at Gate One," a voice announced over the loudspeaker, without apology for the two-hour delay.

"I hate flying," Leslie piped up. "I'm claustrophobic."

"What other imaginary diseases do you have?" Jason teased. "You couldn't get on a plane if you were claustrophobic."

Oblivious to his remark, Leslie muttered, "My psychiatrist says it has something to do with the position in the womb."

"Yeah," Jason sniped. "You fell out, on your head, and you've never been the same since." Leslie saw that Holly was trying to hide a snicker behind Jason's shoulder.

"Look," their mother said, trying to deflect the tension, "if I could do things over I probably would be a different and better mother. But *that*—the womb—there is nothing I could do to change that."

"At least you could have wallpapered it," Leslie joked.

"Very funny," her mother said, biting her lip to hold back a smile.

The supervisor reappeared to escort them through a private door into the first-class section of the plane. Leslie watched other tourists file past the family. She wished she could do something respectable, like fall in love with the young doctor-type whose clean fingers plucked the strings of his tennis racket, but knew she desired someone more compelling, creative. All the Jewish professionals, the lawyers, doctors, their wives and kids, had drizzly December expressions. Only the WASPs, fresh from their squash and racketball games, looked chipper. At a certain level of Jewishness, the next logical step was WASPdom.

Leslie's father did not wear a pinkie ring or clear nail polish like some of the men in their town, and neither of the daughters liked jewelry. Her mother's diamond ring was always described as "tastefully cut" and often she turned it inside her finger. Yet when Gentiles at the office assumed Leslie was one of them, she turned instantly into Super Jew, closer to WASP than goyim, a whole different species, who had a heyday with costume jewelry.

A man with a paunch hanging over the beltline of his turquoise-checkered trousers struggled with a box that kept getting stuck in the aisle. Trim men in pinstriped suits never seemed to have such trouble. No doubt he was on a gambling junket, and Leslie was glad that her family always stayed at secluded beach resorts with steel bands for evening entertainment. Eight bars of "Yellow Bird" could cause someone to lose her mind, but never her shirt, as it were.

The forward section of the plane looked like the reading room of the local library. Leslie's father was always complaining, after a flight, about the feckless talk around him. "They don't read," he would grunt. "These morons!" In addition to their books, each child had his or her own newspaper, refusing to share one copy. The love had been split three ways, and they relished separate possessions as a consolation prize for their parents' busy professional schedules. Her father constantly reminded them, "Have I ever cheated you? You all get the same." But in the same moment he peeled off hundred-dollar bills and instructed their mother, "I want you to divide it among the girls. Jason—that's his problem." The daughters, each successful in her own right, aggressively pleaded for a genderless division of money.

Leslie peeked over her book at the flight attendant doing her stand-up subliminal-panic routine about possible lack of oxygen in the cabin. The stewardess breathed into a yellow plastic cone that hung from a licorice-whip cord attached to the overhead compartment. Then she came up for more hot air before lurching like a drunk into her seat for the takeoff. Bravo. Encore.

Leslie counted to ten as the plane roared down the runway and off the ground. If she could reach that number, then she would be safe. Whenever the plane bumped she went through the same routine, only faster and faster, depending on the size of the air pockets. Turbulence always seemed to arrive with the meal. Then Leslie fantasized her camp counselor role, rounding everybody up for a safe evacuation.

The jumbo jet banked over the bay as though squatting, too close to the water, it seemed. Then the big bird lifted itself up and the "No Smoking" sign was turned off, matches lit and blown out, the smell of burning human flesh still in Leslie's psyche. After two years, she still could not forget the crash she had covered sloshing through filthy waters, treading over dismembered limbs, to interview a survivor, still strapped into his seat and floating in the papier-mâché debris of the plane. As so often happened, tragedy got Leslie's heart started up again, jolted her out of numbness.

A white tablecloth was spread over a food tray with heavy, gleaming pieces of silverware on top of it. Leslie decided to forgo the cocktail, not because of the hour of the morning but to cut down on trips to the toilet. Though fastidious to the point of showering twice a day, she never washed her hands in airplane bathrooms. There was not enough time to urinate—in spurts because of her nerves—wash up, and get back to her seat in time to prepare for a crash landing. Crouching over the toilet seat, she held the door shut with one arm against it. She stopped long enough to flush the toilet only when she had her period. In second grade Leslie stood guard like a stern matron in the Girls' Room and reported on kids who whisked out the door without stopping at the sink. She marveled at their nonchalance and could never understand why they did not have guilty consciences. Always the offenders were the prettiest and most popular girls, and Leslie would tell everyone they were just sneaks, filthy ones at that.

She poked at the limp eggs and greasy purplish sausage and then drank the glass of orange juice on the tray. The plane, wrapped in yellow mist, shuddered as though riding on a rope full of knots. Last summer Leslie and her mother had flown back from Europe in a thunderstorm. She had never known how to tell her mother that she loved her best of all. Inventing a story about a crash, Leslie said she would pull her mother out first, before any other relative or lover. "I'm not so sure," her mother challenged with a coy smile. "After all, I'm much older. I've lived my life." Leslie winced.

The aircraft seemed to hang in a gray mass of clouds and the whine of its dragging engines made her nervous. Static came over the cabin address system, and Leslie clutched her armrest in preparation for an announcement.

Out came a melodic voice. "Please be seated, ladies and gentlemen. We be start our show, Fashions Aloft." A flight attendant in a swimsuit emerged from the tiny bathroom and waltzed down the aisle. "Now, dis is lovely Marva in a strapless suit from Carom's Shop in downtown Anlucia, your guide to resort living." The hostess, another flight attendant, narrated. Everyone clapped. Marva changed into three more outfits before the show was over.

Was this a spoof? Leslie wondered. Here they were, 32,000 feet up and probably passing over Washington, D.C., just digging out from under a near-blizzard, and this flight attendant-cum-model was parading around the cabin half-naked. A smile replaced Leslie's glum expression. She adored these islanders, for being so silly and also so unconcerned about convention.

34

With the show ended, Leslie slipped back into her gloom. She wrapped herself in a short blanket to ward off the chill in the cabin and pressed her face into the hollow of the tiny window to hide her tears.

"What are you watching?" Rebecca nudged her. "You can't see anything out there but clouds."

"Oh, I'm just making sure that nothing happens."

"You're *making* me nervous."

"Then don't look."

"You're impossible." Rebecca sulked. "Jerk."

Slumping in her seat, Leslie thought how she wanted to be going in a different direction, to California, to spend the holiday with Adam. But for the moment she was unwanted on his turf. He had often berated her for going away with her family. She had almost canceled out once before just to please him. If Leslie told Adam her whereabouts at this moment, then surely there would be no chance for reconciliation. Instead, she went along, on the theory that she would not be tempted to call or write, in order to keep that information from him.

Rebecca, suddenly turned jovial, poked Leslie out of deep thought. "Daddy is in the paper for a case," she said, giving a scattered commentary on what she read. "Oh, my God, you should see this character who's coming into his court."

"Who?" Leslie leaned over to look at the story. Her younger sister's speech was often difficult to follow, a dialect of half-starts and staccato sentences.

⁻Rebecca tightened her grip on the newspaper, pulling it over her nose like a sun visor. "You have your own paper," she scolded.

At all times she asserted a territorial imperative that seemed limitless, extending from her purse to a towel in the bathroom and even to the glove compartment of a rental car.

Wearily, Leslie bent down to lift her newspaper from the floor. She turned to the page Rebecca was guarding and read:

ATTORNEY SEEKS DISMISSAL OF
TAX CASE AGAINST REPUTED MOBSTER

by Arthur T. Berens

The attorney for reputed organized crime leader Joseph Pugliasi said yesterday that he will ask for a dismissal of a tax fraud indictment on the grounds that his client was denied a speedy trial.

"It is wrong for defendants to be under a cloud of indictment for an unreasonable period of time," defense attorney Norman A. Kahn said. "My client's constitutional right to a speedy trial is being violated."

The case against Mr. Pugliasi, free on a $50,000 recognizance bond, is scheduled to be heard January 6 by Federal Court Judge Theodore Rittman.

More than a year has passed since the 62-year-old Pugliasi was indicted by a federal jury on charges of filing a false income tax return for 1975. The Speedy Trial Act, enacted by Congress in 1974, allows dismissal of federal charges against a person not brought to trial within 100 days of his arrest. Informed by the Constitution's Sixth Amendment, the Act gives a judge discretion to decide whether the same charges could later be filed against the defendant.

Twice the prosecution sought and was granted postponements of the trial. The case was believed to be weakened after Assistant U.S. Attorney Matt Sonnett permitted two potential witnesses to leave the jurisdiction prior to the issuance of subpoenas. Despite efforts to track them down, the two men have not been heard from since and are believed to have fled the country.

In 1975, the prosecution charges, Mr. Pugliasi spent more than $150,000 on renovations and additions to his beachfront home in Montauk, on Long Island's posh East

End, while reporting an income of only $35,000 for that same year.

Police intelligence sources say Mr. Pugliasi is acting boss of the organization known to police and federal authorities as the Rastellano crime family, after its first leader, Carmen Rastellano.

Authorities believe that even behind bars Mr. Pugliasi would be capable of exercising leadership over a criminal empire whose illegal activities include narcotics, gambling, truck hijacking, loansharking and labor racketeering. According to a 1973 internal report of the New York City Police Department, the organization, with tentacles reaching into many states, Canada and the Caribbean, "controls the large majority of heroin shipped through Canada to the United States."

Despite a long record of arrests Mr. Pugliasi has never been convicted of a major crime. If found guilty of tax fraud, he could receive up to a $20,000 fine and 10 years in prison or both.

"This Mr. Pugliasi seems like a very nice person," Leslie said. She was amused now, imagining the courtroom dialogue between this thug and her father, whose sky-blue eyes were as pristine as his mind.

"I dunno, Judge, what I'm doing here."

"I know why I'm here," her father would reply, his permanently furrowed brow projecting a fierce intelligence. "But if you do not know why you're here, then I suggest you consult with your attorney before you try practicing law on your own behalf."

Leslie looked up from her paper and saw passengers stretching and walking in the aisle in their stocking feet. A father held on to the overhead compartment, his armpit visible through an opening in his short-sleeved shirt, pulling out pillows and blankets and dropping them on his wife's and children's laps. Leslie's father used to ride planes like taxicabs, but she had only flown with him a half-dozen times. He chuckled over her terror, explaining how rubber bands held the aircraft together.

The plane looked as though it would bang against a float of clouds up ahead, but glided through them, a gossamer of milky air racing by. Leslie put on cloth eyeshades to blot out the celestial landscape. Soon tears trickled out of the corners of them, blurring a wistful vision of Adam poised at the bottom of the staircase as she stepped off the plane. She remembered their first date, six months ago, the night of the blackout, when she had finally given up on his coming. By nine o'clock at night, with both airports shut down, Leslie had changed out of a dress and into a nightgown. Moments later there came a knock at the door. Leslie looked through the peephole and saw Adam's oblong face, the milk chocolate eyes lighted by a candle he held in front of his nose. She opened the door and he stood in the hallway blowing out a stump of melting candle and huffing. "I wouldn't have missed this for anything. The lights went out the minute after we landed. Whew! I ran and got a taxi. I had the driver wait while I dropped my bags at the hotel and then raced over here. Some bozo in your lobby wouldn't let me up because the elevators aren't working. I grabbed a candle from the desk and ran up the six flights."

"Would you like to come in?" Leslie inquired amusedly.

"Sure," Adam said, his eyes twinkling.

She fixed him a drink and they sat in the darkened living room, with headlights from cars outside sending streamers through the window.

Adam looked better than she remembered him from a San Francisco gallery opening she had covered a few weeks before for her magazine. He had long eyelashes which made him seem sensitive, a downturned, sultry lower lip and hands with bent-back thumbs he said were good for ringing doorbells, but which Leslie thought of as sculpture. She left for New York the next morning, and he tracked her down at the office to ask her out the first chance he got to come east, to show his paintings.

Leslie remembered she was wearing only a nightgown under her robe. "I usually don't greet men . . ."

"I like your bathrobe." He beamed. There was nothing lascivious about the remark, only a niceness, and she was comfortable enough to change in the bedroom while Adam waited in the living room. She felt light-headed, buoyed by Adam's ambition and eagerness to be with her. They rode to dinner in a hansom cab, graced by lanterns, and then talked until dawn about their life plans, where they had come from and were headed, together. It was understood even then.

Her heart thumped so loudly that it kept her awake. But soon the heaviness in Leslie's head, swollen with tears, forced sleep on her.

It must have been a good two hours before she woke up. A flight attendant tapped her lightly on the shoulder, and Leslie groped for her seatbelt before removing the eyeshades. She felt an undertow of doom as she sailed into layers of clouds below, finally emerging into sunshine and blue skies. The jet swooped low, its wings wiggling, over the clear blue waters speckled with golden sun drops.

"Ladies and gentlemen, we are now making our approach into Anlucia," the pilot announced in his best monotone. "The weather is eighty-five degrees and clear. We hope you have enjoyed your flight with us and hope to see you all again soon. And Merry Christmas to you, folks."

Leslie no longer wanted to watch the landing, something that normally gave her relief and pleasure. Now it could only be a letdown. In transit she had held onto a hope that Adam might show up on the island. So obsessed with endings, Leslie found the arrival of the flight had an unaccustomed poignancy and sadness, merging into and blurring any feeling of excitement about the start of the holiday.

3

A dusty white jeep sped under the wing of the plane as the family spilled onto the steamy tarmac. One man in a print gauze shirt drove while the other, his feet propped on top of the windshield, held a huge transistor radio to his ear. Transistors were the new status symbol of the downtrodden on New York streets. Was it possible that Leslie's grocery boy, fleeing the cold, was now in that jeep? If so, Leslie would shriek, "I came here to get away from you," just like the New York grandmother whose hand ex-Mayor Lindsay had tried to shake in Miami Beach during his aborted presidential drive.

At the outdoor arrivals area, the people hugging, sobbing and clutching one another looked to be the same ones Leslie had seen waving goodbye, with wadded tissues, five hours earlier at Kennedy Airport. She wondered how they got here so fast.

Puffs of humid air swirled around Leslie, causing an

itching sensation. She tucked her wool crew-neck sweater into the arm of her raincoat and rolled up her shirtsleeves. Her ears, still stuffed from the plane ride, registered a distant surf sound. The abrupt change from winter to summer left her floating in a neverland. The cold, for which she suddenly longed, seemed to be more definite.

Leslie, fitting in nowhere, always wanted to be some other place. Her existence was like the small, almost imperceptible center of a paper doily, embroidered with elegant dinner parties and opening nights, the life of celebrity journalism, not her own. There were too many rough edges to her personality.

Her mother, in an impeccably tailored tan pants-suit, led the way, with her walking medicine chest stowed in a carry-on cosmetics case. She still brought baby powder, barrettes, eye drops, laxatives and antihistamines on the assumption, often correct, that her children had forgotten an item. Until her thirtieth birthday Leslie had been a functional illiterate with car insurance and medical forms, which her mother had always impatiently snatched out of her hand and promptly filled out. Leslie's mother, whose only foray into the well-staffed kitchen of her home was to burn chocolate chip cookies, was often astonished at her children's lack of practicality and domesticity.

As they entered the tiny manila-colored terminal, her mother told them to sit while she waited on line at Customs. Leslie was charmed by the freshly painted blue booth that looked more like a lemonade stand than an official entry point. Whenever the baggage inspector would mark her suitcase with an *X*, signaling his okay, Leslie was always tempted to scribble *O*, just like in the game tick-tack-toe. The island invoked memories of a childhood that was indelible.

"Good to see you bahk, my lady," the Customs officer

said, gently taking the passports out of her mother's hand and stamping them all in one motion.

Leslie was proud of her mother's appearance, the natural gray hair falling into neat layers, sharp brown eyes and chin, head slightly tilted, awaiting questions with an understated eagerness, commanding respect. Some of the housewives in their town looked like drag queens, with straw hair piled high on top of their heads, clown makeup and anorectic bodies zipped into Gloria Vanderbilt jeans.

At the baggage carrousel the family was observed, not for their good looks, but for their air of wealth. A hefty man with a fried-chicken yellowish complexion and pitch-black sunglasses stuck a flyer advertising free casino chips under Leslie's arm. Uncreasing her elbow, she let the sheet of paper sail to the ground to leave herself free to help with the bags.

Filling in for her father, who would not allow anyone to lift a finger around the airport, Leslie often served as the aide-de-camp to her mother on trips. A strong body qualified her for the role. By the time Jason was old enough to lend a hand, Leslie was reluctant to delegate any work to him. She made preemptive moves in all areas of her life. At the office Leslie typed her own letters for fear that a secretary might misspell a word or misjudge a margin. She stayed late to get out her correspondence, much as she had copied her homework over a dozen times when she was a child. Such a take-charge stance was not easily relinquished, and she felt comfortably in control.

Leslie lifted each bag onto the still conveyor and waited for the Customs inspector to pick a target. His fingertips were smudged, and she worried that in thumbing through her belongings he might soil her tennis whites. She still found it funny when an inspector ferreted a stray tampon out of her suitcase. Now he selected her mother's cosmetics case. These guys were trained to sniff out the junkie. Unzipping the brown canvas, he shuffled the articles like dice and randomly landed on a bottle of Tuinals. Staring vacantly at the prescription label, he twirled the bottle in his hand, placed it back in the case and then waved the family through an open door onto a palm-fringed parking lot no larger or more attractive than a sand lot.

The taxi driver, dubbed Shinehead for his shiny bald pate, greeted them. Instead of bowing and curtseying to tourists, locals adopted nicknames that had a magical effect on the tourists' pocketbook. They also gave up-to-the-minute weather reports of uninterrupted sunshine for the whole month while navigating a puddle in the road. As Shinehead lifted bags onto the top rack of his taxi, he listened absently to instructions from Leslie's mother about picking them up the last day. She had called him from New York ahead of time, and now she was telling him to check in their bags on the morning of their final day and later deliver the family to the airport. Leslie felt as if she were suffocating in details.

"My husband is coming in Monday night," her mother persisted. "You better check and see that the plane is on time, please."

"Yes, ma'am," Shinehead said, his attention focused on a piece of rope he used to strap the bags to an overhead rack.

"Eastern," she said. "Flight Twenty-four."

"Shinehead can't pick us up next Christmas," Leslie alerted her mother. "He has a funeral to attend."

"What?" Holly piped up. "How could he know so far in advance?"

"Well, next year he's planning to murder the first tourist who plagues him with these kinds of details."

The family piled into the cab, and Leslie opened the window to let the soft night air in. A trade wind picking up force along the dark open fields just past the makeshift cemetery shredded Rebecca's long straight hair into frizzled strands.

"Close the window," she commanded. "I'm getting that Airedale look."

Leslie rolled up the window, deferring to the air conditioner. A hint of island atmosphere came out of the car radio, playing Calypso songs. She looked ahead at the stars, already old in the sky. The hillside rose up in rough stalks of weeds. A ramshackle wood-frame house, with a broken screen where a front door should have been, was barely visible through a forest of palm and fig trees. In many instances the foliage was more imposing than the houses. Baby goats curled up on dirt patches outside. A fat cow swishing its tail waddled across the dark road, causing Shinehead to pump his brakes down hard. A roadside bar, virtually deserted, had empty wooden cases of sodas pushed against the wall. Bare-chested boys, with shimmering mahogany skins lighted by Shinehead's high beams, shuffled home in worn-out thongs.

Shortly they passed a group of churches. Leslie imagined their wooden pews filled with young boys in clean white shirts and women in straw hats. A spray of stars sprinkled over the area, brightening the road.

"We just be passing All Saints Town," Shinehead announced. "Of course now and den dere may be deh devil waiting in dah road. Even if you be good, he could meet you later."

Moments later Shinehead made a sharp left, his car wobbling over a pebbled driveway that sloped down to the hotel by the sea. The sound of taxi doors opening and closing magnified the stillness of the night. A few islanders leaned against parked rental cars or sat sleepily on the curb. A young black, no more than sixteen, steered a baggage cart over to a car. As he worked, stacking the suitcases symmetrically, he made almost no sound.

Inside the covered area of the gingerbread building, a Midwestern matron sat holding together the ribbon-bound edges of the white angora sweater that draped her shoulders. A white patent-leather pocketbook with an oversized gold snap sat on her lap. The hotel bulletin board that stood on wooden legs announced the appearance of Sugar's Combo in white block letters. There was the scraping of chairs against the stone floors as people got up from tables to dance. Others sat languidly on the terrace and sipped after-dinner drinks.

"Good to hav you with us again," the smiling desk clerk said, setting down a pile of name-and-address index cards before them. "How is dah fahmily?"

"Fine," Leslie's mother said proudly.

A balding man in khaki trousers and a pink Lacoste shirt interrupted to ask about an urgent call he was expecting from New York. His little daughter, in an ankle-length pink dress, trotted around him in white patent-leather Mary Janes with matching cotton socks. People came to the island to get away from it all, as it were, but needed to stay in touch with their offices to feel worthwhile. If Leslie ever achieved any artistic success, the only kind that mattered, she would put the world on hold, without the benefit of canned music, and forget about it for a few days.

"Go and have a drink," Leslie's mother said, figuring out room assignments.

"I'll wait with you, Mom," Jason said, his wife in tow.

The bar seemed to be staked out by the locals, distinguished from the native islanders by both their skin color and avid drinking. Despite the curative effects of the salty air and sea, they had a bruised look about them. The sun burned crinkly lines into the napes of their necks and their brittle blondish leg hairs looked twined with sand. Their trademark outfit was Bermuda shorts, a broadcloth shirt worn outside and buffalo sandals dried out like rotting meat. Most of them appeared to dabble in real estate, pitching to tourists over a few martinis. This was their proverbial last resort, and having come this far, the next step was to allow the sea to claim them. Perhaps Leslie's loneliness would be lost in the frivolity that characterized their drinking bouts.

Leslie and Rebecca ordered rum swizzles, as was their custom on arrival. Their favorite bartender, Wellington, was on duty. He had sparkling white fingernails, the hue of a seashell, and kept them immaculate by dipping his hands in ice. He gave them doubles.

"Where's Guy?" Rebecca snickered as she referred to the French manager. Every island resort had one of his ilk, direct from the Charles Boyer school of personal charm, with the low, sexy European accent like a wiggle. Guy had a cleft chin and thinning blond hair that reminded her of Aschenbach. But in his Bermuda shorts and high socks he sometimes seemed an effeminate little boy.

"Mr. Guy is off the island," the bartender said. "He be bahk in a few days."

"Mister?" Rebecca said playfully.

"*Master* Guy," he said, winking at her.

Everyone knew Guy was quite fey, but there was further speculation about him. Discreetly, he worked over wealthy widows and divorcées and accepted invitations to their European villas when the hotel shut down in summer. He was careful to book these women into the place at separate times. But one year, two admirers showed up the same week. At the risk of offending one of his ardent female sponsors, he took Leslie, who had a teenage crush on him, to the annual Policemen's Ball on the island. Other evenings he retired early, evoking sympathy from these women about his epilepsy.

Guy claimed to have acquired the disease after a robber hit him over the head with a gun during a holdup. Another version that more people tended to believe was that his homosexual lover had caught Guy in bed with one of the black waiters. Infuriated about Guy's alleged sexual preference, Leslie begged a waiter to take her to the local gay bar to catch him in the act. Rebecca went along for the fun of it. All they could find out was that no one there had ever heard of Guy or seen anyone resembling him.

Their mother walked over to the bar and ordered a scotch to take to the back of the room. She informed them that there had been a mix-up and there was only one rondavel, a thatched cottage right on the beach, at the moment. Jason and Holly, she said, would be occupying it.

"Why them?" Rebecca protested. "I wanted that room."

"Tomorrow some people are checking out," her mother said. "They'll move you into another rondavel."

"I have more things than Jason," she persisted. "My sketch pads and brushes . . ."

"They'll carry your clothes on hangers," her mother said, trying to appease Rebecca.

"Why should Jason get the room tonight?"

"We asked for it," Jason explained. "Holly and I told Mommy to be sure to reserve one for us months ago."

"Holly's not even part of this family," Rebecca sniped.

"What are you talking about?" he shot back. "Holly's my wife."

"She's still not part of the family," Rebecca insisted. "Take her on your own vacation. Why should Mommy and Daddy have to pay for her? If you love her so much . . ."

"Stop it," her mother pleaded.

"No," Jason insisted. "I want to get this straightened out, now."

"Jason," his wife whispered, squeezing his hand, "drop it." Holly possessed a strong will, but managed to appear conciliatory, quietly so, just as long as she got her own way.

"Okay. I'm going to my room," Mrs. Rittman sighed. "I'm exhausted."

In the past, Leslie and Rebecca had always shared a room because they liked to go out on the town. But in recent times Leslie preferred to stay in and read. Jason used to sleep on a cot in their room, but was evicted as soon as he started to touch himself. They gave as a reason his impossible habit of never blowing his nose and driving them crazy with his sniffling.

Inside the cottage Leslie unpacked her suitcase, which she put on top of the bed next to the window. The cold stone floors, with a small worn turquoise rug between the beds, and cheap wooden bureau drawers made the room look lonely, cast off. Leslie tried to ward off an emptiness by imposing her personal belongings on the room—books on a shelf, a hairbrush in front of the mirror, clothes in a closet. She thought of Graham Greene's advice, as an African traveler, to wait and let a few days pass and the strange would become the heart of the familiar.

Leslie was inconsolable. No matter where she went, even with the family, she couldn't re-create the feeling of security she had had as a child. Whenever she went on a business or pleasure trip she felt as if she were back in Grand Central Station, lining up in uniform with an olive canteen case strapped on her shoulder. Sending Leslie to summer camp at eight was something like hatching an egg too soon. The baby chick could not survive. Leslie never got over it. She even felt homesick in her own apartment.

Still livid, Rebecca sat at the edge of her bed and complained about Holly. "Who the hell does she think she is? She's so pushy. She's not even part of this family."

"We'll be moved tomorrow," Leslie responded. Vulnerable to Rebecca's perceptions and often swayed by them, she tried to veer away from the subject of their sister-in-law. Leslie also thought of her as a Johnny-come-lately who

49

maybe should never have arrived in the first place. The family was a fortress, impenetrable to outsiders, even those who thought they had a key to gain access. The emotional combinations of the clan changed from day to day, hour to hour.

"That's not the point," Rebecca said. "Mommy gives in to her."

"You're imagining that."

"No, I'm not," said Rebecca, now pacing the room in a fury. "That girl is too much. Now she'll have this baby, and we'll be stuck with her."

"She's Jason's wife not yours."

Unheeding, Rebecca predicted that the baby would be deformed and ugly. Holly had come from a poor family, but as an only child was given the benefits of a superior education and a large wardrobe. Her parents had sacrificed everything for her, and both had died premature deaths.

"If that's the case," Leslie said, "they'll give the baby up for adoption."

"No they won't," Rebecca said, wrinkling her face with disgust. "You know Mommy and Daddy—they'll take care of that kid."

"You're wrong," Leslie said. "You know how Daddy even hates it when someone is fat or has pimples."

"She has bad blood," Rebecca explained. "I don't want hers mixed with ours. She's polluting the family." Sometimes Rebecca's theories rivaled those of Lillian the cook, who canceled a trip to Detroit one Christmas after reading in Art Buchwald's column that Michigan was being moved to Arkansas.

Still, Leslie had a feeling about finding the right blood donor as a mate. Her father had convinced her that by some genetic miracle no one in the family was prone to heart attacks, bad skin, cancer or dying in plane crashes. "We don't have a history of this in our family," he proclaimed.

Leslie felt she owed it to him to find someone who was the right type. Yet no one seemed to match up to what he wanted for his daughters. A poor person was unacceptable, but so was a millionaire textile manufacturer who moved his hands too much when he talked. Doctors were too unidimensional in her father's mind.

"Rebecca, why not make Holly take a blood oath?" Leslie joked. The family was, in fact, tight like the Mafia. They even had their own special communication code, mostly free association, difficult for outsiders to follow and spoken in a frantic trying-to-get-one-word-in-at-the-dinner-table rhythm.

"You think I'm kidding," she said, refusing to be sidetracked from a cause that was fast becoming her own special mania. "There's bad blood."

"Maybe," Leslie suggested, "they'll get lucky with the baby. Right now I want to go to bed." She took off her clothes, damp from perspiration, and rolled them into her empty suitcase. Then she went into the bathroom to shower and brush her teeth.

"I'm going to get a soda," Rebecca said. "I'll unpack tomorrow." As she opened the door, a trade wind swept cool blue jacaranda blossoms into the room. Scooping them up gently in her hands, Rebecca savored their sweetness. Then she stepped over a stray coconut, with its monkey face, on the patio. Brushing it aside with her foot, she muttered, "That Holly really hit the jackpot marrying into our family."

4

Leslie woke in a sweat, as if from a bad dream. Her top sheet hung from the mattress onto the floor. She had probably kicked it off in the middle of the night. The air conditioner, slightly lopsided in the wall, was off. Its rattling might disturb the dawn rehearsal of the yellow birds. But seeing that Rebecca was already gone from the room, Leslie figured it must be after ten by now.

A knock at the door summoned her to breakfast on the patio. The day was gorgeous, with a linen-blue sky and a soft breeze blowing off the sea. Dotting the beach were thatched white cottages framed by poincianas and hibiscuses. Leslie looked at her plate. She liked the blend of chilled honeydew and cantaloupe melons with the pastel tones of the island.

She savored the breakfast, something she avoided back home. The morning papers and coffee in a styrofoam cup awaited her at the office. The breakfast table did not belong to a woman who was alone. It was a place where some freckle-faced kid ditched his spoon in a lump of hot oatmeal cereal on the pretext of having to catch the school bus, a father took baby sips of coffee to avoid soiling his white shirt, and the wife belted a terry-cloth robe as she rose from the table to freshen the pot. Missing breakfast was skipping out on a part of life that Leslie did not care to face that early in the day.

Once she had been offered a breakfast arrangement that might have seemed the perfect solution. Señor Carlos Rodriguez, a Harvard-educated banker, divorced and ten years older, offered a room to Leslie in his Waldorf-Astoria suite on the sole condition that she have breakfast with him every morning. "I'm worried about you," he said. "Your life is too frantic. You rush by it."

He was not imperceptive. In a hurry to start her career, Leslie left after her last college exam, not waiting for commencement, to answer an advertisement for an English-language daily in San Juan, Puerto Rico. She talked the editor into hiring her and, on ninety dollars a week, rented a room from an old lady in a walk-up without an air conditioner. Determined to make it on her own, she refused repeated offers of help from her parents.

Toward the end of the summer stint she met Carlos on a story. Driven and high-powered, he saw the same qualities in Leslie and tried to tame them. Carlos was attractive, with shiny black eyes, a prematurely graying crewcut, slightly buck teeth, like a rabbit, when he smiled, squatty, but virile in the brain. Yet Leslie could never bring herself to sleep with him, though she enjoyed his strong, definite embrace and the fresh aroma of his laundered shirts laced with a light lemon after-shave. He followed Leslie back to New York, where he made the breakfast offer, only to be rebuffed again.

Shortly thereafter Leslie found her way into the bed of an

Irish writer, married and about one hundred pounds over-weight. Pete gorged himself on her as though she were strawberry shortcake. Six months later, when the plate was licked clean and he ran out of promises about leaving the wife when his son graduated from college, his pushed her aside. Irishmen apparently took a longer time than Jewish husbands, whose cut-off date was moved up to a son's Bar Mitzvah. When it was over, Pete lay on the motel bed, puffing on one of the nonfilter cigarettes that put rust stains on his fingertips. "Get some breakfast," he sighed, without meeting her moist eyes. "You'll feel better." That was the last word she ever heard from him.

She kept reviewing the masochism of that relationship, still numb from the pain. It was like wiggling a loose tooth, not being able to keep her tongue and fingers away from it. Nearly ten years had passed, Leslie realized, and this was the first time she had thought about Carlos. Somewhere in her closet, beneath stacks of photographs, there was a pic-ture of them at opening night of the Sammy Davis, Jr., show at the El San Juan Hotel. Carlos took her there again, al-ways reserving the best table, when Rebecca visited the island. He would have done anything for Leslie, and this was already too much. She led Carlos on and eventually wore him out with her indifference.

Leslie got up and walked onto the beach. The rest of the family were already there. Each year her mother hired a beachboy to line up enough chairs and pull them off to a private patch of beach. He tied the chairs together with colored rags, like flags claiming a territory. The local news-paper that had arrived with the breakfast flew out of Les-lie's hands like a kite. She scrambled to halt its flight and folded it under the mat in front of her chair. Sunglasses gave her vertigo, and she could only read when she lay on her stomach with the sun massaging her back. Rubbing suntan cream into her skin, Leslie thought how much she disdained men who had gobs of lotion, like oil slicks, stuck to hairy arms and legs, and pinkish white sunblock on their lips. It was too much like a fetish, worse than a vanity. She closed her eyes and saw yellow dots, which she counted like sheep until she slept.

Leslie felt a poke in her ribs.

"Mommy says you'll burn up," Rebecca warned.

"Jesus, I'm thirty years old."

"She doesn't want you to overdo it the first day," Rebecca persisted. "Remember how swollen my face got two years ago."

"Where is Mommy?"

"She's taking the first of her hundred tennis lessons this week," Jason remarked. His tone was prep-school smart-ass, but he had learned the line from his father, who might just as easily, Leslie thought, have been talking about him. Slightly more coordinated than his mother, Jason made a lot of points on fierce concentration and a driving will. The way he snapped his ankles when he walked reminded Leslie of a penguin.

She had tried unsuccessfully to mold her only brother into an athlete. Beginning with acrobatics when he was four, she taught him somersaults and flips. Lying on her back, she raised her arms and legs, balancing Jason on them and bouncing him around. Exhausted and giggling, they collapsed in each other's arms and fell asleep until it was time for breakfast. Later on Leslie ran spring training for him in the backyard, but Jason was a hopeless case. He was kicked off the school team as a relief outfielder, and Leslie beat up the boy responsible for that decision. She liked to watch Jason do his penmanship homework though, admiring the fact that he was a lefty.

She mourned his growing up. When Jason reached puberty Leslie, passing by his room and seeing the door shut, went directly to bed and masturbated at the thought of the jar of Vaseline he kept in his room. She liked his build, the chubby chest with virtually no hair on it. He resembled the boys she had always been attracted to in high school. Despite her own athleticism, Leslie was drawn to heavy men with soft rolls of flesh, bodies not unlike a woman's. Pete had vestiges of breasts. Other lovers were flabby European Jewish Intellectual Swiss Gnomes with beltlines up to their chests.

Leslie walked over to the tennis court to watch her mother and applaud at the appropriate moments. Too shy to play with strangers, meaning anyone outside the family, her mother opted for lessons. The game lifted her out of her periodic depressions and gave some bounce to her sedentary ways.

A close friend of Leslie's ran what they jokingly called the "menopause clinic" for women who had sidelined it for years, parading around the courts in swimsuits and stacked heels and not wanting to take up the game. The sessions had proved to be as effective as any consciousness-raising group. If these women could wield a racket, then maybe they had other untapped energies. The trouble, though, was that some of them got divorced and their alimony did not cover the tennis clinic. Her friend's get-rich-quick scheme folded like a wilted wedding flower. Many women the same age as Leslie's mother went back to work and found a personal satisfaction. Sarah Rittman, eminent social worker, was cheated out of this discovery because she already had a successful career.

As a measure of her enthusiasm, her mother had invited the teaching pro, a Texan woman about Leslie's age, to their tennis court at the house.

"Your mom's doing great," she had told the children.

Her mother had smiled in disbelief. For years she had sat at the family pool and watched the children play tennis. At any mention of taking up the game, her husband smirked and said, "You're not going to start playing at your age. Don't be ridiculous." When she finally got up the courage, she took lessons faithfully and developed her form. Leslie's father played like a baseball batter but rarely missed a ball, owing to his competitive spirit. The idea of anyone teaching him anything was beyond his grasp. Yet when no one was looking he copied the way Leslie scooped up a ball by pushing a racket against the side of her sneaker. Fearful that her father might suffer a heart attack on the court, Leslie feigned exhaustion to get him to quit.

"Do you want to have lunch now?" her mother asked as she came off the court.

"I guess so."

Her mother wanted everyone at the dinner table promptly at eight and spent the afternoon reminding them. Lunch was more leisurely, and they took advantage of this by strolling in and out like customers at a diner. One replaced another at the table, and no one looked up from a book except to order the meal. Yet like robots they all headed for the same table, sometimes pulling an extra chair up to make room for the latest one to arrive. Only a traitor, Leslie felt, would sit at another table. Next to them, two couples recommended the same boat trip to each other. Their gold wedding bands were all gleaming and new, marking them as honeymooners, who always seemed to group in fours.

"I heard Chris Evert is on the island," Jason said as he got up from the table.

"Where?" Her mother always liked to discover that other prominent persons—as she and her husband were described in the newspapers—frequented the same resort. It gave her a goose bump of self-importance that Chris Evert might right now be working out with the same pro from whom she had just taken a lesson.

"Right at this table," Jason said, breaking up with laughter. "In *your* seat."

When their mother went swimming she was cheered on by her children. "Go, Esther Williams, go!" Protected by a bathing cap, she did not hear them and kept stroking away. Once out of the water she wanted to know what they found so funny. "It's nothing, Esther," they invariably replied.

She relished the gentle teasing, which seemed to bring out the little girl in her. At the outset of her marriage she had been a superb horseback rider, but her athletic prowess diminished over the space of five years in which she gave birth to three children. Now her attempts at sports had the aspect of buffoonery, which along with a gall bladder operation inspired a rare romantic response from her husband. Had the children's joking been instead a slight she would not have recognized it as such. Having no meanness inside her, she tended to overlook any possible unkindnesses directed against her. Competent and conscientious about her career, she did not have time, like some indolent housewife, for marathon phone conversations about the latest snub at the country club, to which the family would never belong in the first place. They had their inside jokes, not to be shared with a stranger on the next mat at a club pool.

Leslie ordered a rum swizzle to take back to the room and stopped by the front desk to collect some stationery. Settling into a desk chair, she took a sip of the cool drink and looked to the sea for consolation. Her body tensed up and her head became heavy, as though waterlogged, while she strained to find words to draw Adam back. The scene was disturbingly familiar: Leslie off in a room somewhere, shutting out the life of the moment, in order to conduct some secret little seduction on paper to resurrect a dead romance. Carrying a torch for someone was one thing, but staying indoors on a beautiful day composing letters to fan the flame was a bit much. Leslie had done this too many times in the past and then berated herself for it. She refused to surrender the day to someone who was probably not even thinking of her. Putting the stationery in a desk drawer, to give herself something to look forward to, she fled the room.

She decided to water-ski and walked to the far end of the beach, in the opposite direction from the family, to book time. At Shorty the King of Calypso's Watersports concession, a primitive wooden shack, a couple of teenagers stood around, corn-rowing their hair. It occurred to Leslie that in all her Christmases on the island she had never seen Shorty in the daylight. Nor could she recall ever catching one of his performances. Nonetheless, Shorty was a star and could hardly be expected to rent snorkels and fins to tourists on the beach. Though most guests at the hotels where he performed were asleep by midnight, Shorty the King of Calypso left word with his personal staff that he was never to be awakened before noon.

"So where's Shorty?" Leslie asked.

"He be sleep. He hav big show tonight."

A teenager skipped into the water, waving Leslie on. He handed her a ski. While he got in a boat and cranked up the engine, she squatted in the water to adjust the ski. He threw out a rope and she treaded water to grab it behind the boat, which was now sputtering gas fumes. The boat moved farther away, and as the rope got taut, Leslie held her breath until she was up. A bellyflop hurt too much. She made it!

Tackling one ski, she zigzagged over the water, jumping in and out of wakes as the salt sprayed her face and hair. Through the wet mist she kept looking in the direction of the family to make sure they were watching her. Now racing parallel to them, she removed one hand from the rope, extending it in a gesture of bravado. Pushing herself, activating muscles untouched in other sports, she strained to make extra turns before letting go and gliding to shore on a tricky wave.

Everyone applauded. Rebecca was the great beauty,

Jason the intellectual, and his wife, Holly, the "she-could-do-no-wrong" honored guest. Leslie found approbation through daring feats.

"You're crazy, Leslie," her brother taunted. "You won't be able to move. If I had skied the first day, I would have quit after one turn."

"You're not me," she said, her teeth chattering.

"Thank God. I'd have to be either an idiot or Evel Knievel, which is probably the same thing."

With his cool logic, Jason often made Leslie feel like a crazed and idiotic person. Now that he had fulfilled his father's dream by getting a Ph.D. in economics, Jason gained status as the resident intellectual. Whereas irrelevancies tended to become Leslie's fascinations, brevity and clarity characterized his thought processes. Often he treated her circumlocutions like a dog sniffing an object and then instantly moving on with a mixture of vague contempt and uninterest. His laugh was like a yelp whenever Leslie did something he considered to be foolish. She was too hurt by his disrespect to express her anger.

Falling down on the chaise longue, Leslie tried to catch her breath while knotting a towel and then drying herself. The pain was bracing, almost invigorating, like a smack of life.

"I think I'll skip dinner, Mom. I'll be too sore to budge."

"You know they've changed your room," she said. "Your things were just moved a few minutes ago to the rondavel."

Rebecca glared at their sister-in-law.

"Leslie, why can't you do things in moderation?" Jason asked in a scolding voice.

Without answering him, Leslie went to her cottage for a shower. Lying on the bed in a towel, she gazed past the muted red lines of sunset. Then she picked up her diary and wrote:

"Jason is a prick."

5

In the morning the battering of tropical rain against the slat windows woke her. Opening one eye, Leslie peeked at the travel alarm clock and saw it was exactly seven in the morning. The phone rang in the room. It was her mother.

"Leslie, what'll I do? Come quickly. Get Rebecca up."

By the time she clicked off, Rebecca was already sitting up in bed, stretching her arms to pull the sleep out of her body.

"Mommy wants us in her room," Leslie announced. "She sounds frantic."

"What is she worried about now?"

"I have no idea."

If their mother had no particular worry on her mind, she invented one. Crossing a busy intersection at rush hour. Locking the car doors. Packing too little in a suitcase. Riding a bicycle after dark. Not having the right pair of shoes for a formal party. "When are you coming out to shop? I'm worried that you won't have a dress for your brother's wedding." Given assurances from the daughters that their blue jeans would be washed and pressed on time, Leslie's mother pushed the alarm button.

"You know, your father and I aren't going to be around forever," she warned. "I don't know what you'll all do."

It was true that the children sometimes appeared helpless. When Leslie's mother started working, she was expected home at six on the button for supper with the children. "Without fail," her husband's voice boomed, "or else, over, finished"—meaning her mother's nascent career. After dinner she was allowed to make speeches on juvenile delinquency and in no time became the "witch doctor to suburban youth." At the office she left instructions to be notified immediately if the children needed her. She moved in and out of meetings like a yo-yo, to field complaints about sore throats, cuts, scratches, flat bike tires and mosquito bites. She had no fear of traveling to remote places or staying in a big old house alone. Instead, she created little panics inside herself, trained as she was to be mindful of minutiae.

Now grown, they still played with her, calling from the cleaners to have her mediate a dispute with the owner over a burned blouse or from a camera store whose sales manager refused to refund the price of a pair of binoculars. "Your mother is in conference," answered her kindly secretary, thinking she was talking to rational adults. "Is it important?" It was hard to know anymore, like trying to figure out why a grown-up still bit her fingernails.

Hurriedly, Leslie grabbed a robe and ran with Rebecca to her mother's cottage. The rest of the family stumbled into the room in various stages of undress. Jason wore only underpants, and his wife, who had grown up in dark city apartments and could not get used to crickets, removed her earplugs. Their mother frantically changed the stations on the tiny transistor radio.

"It's pouring outside," she announced. "Your father is going to blame me."

She lighted a cigarette before crushing out one that was still burning in an ashtray overflowing with bent, half-smoked stalks. Pacing the room, she looked small and fragile, shrunk from her five-foot six-inch frame, in a red polka-dot nightgown. Goose bumps broke out on her arms. Sarah Rittman, erect and composed before admiring suburban audiences, now wrapped her arms around herself as though writhing from a bellyache.

Why was she so afraid of this man, her husband? What could he do? Hang a noose around her neck? Divorce her? Have her injected with a fatal dose of pain-killer? None of the above. What Theodore Rittman did was much more insidious. He infected his wife and children with a belief that they were all inferior and second-rate minds. Then he could come to the rescue, lifting them from their mediocrity. "Morons, idiots, wastrels," he snarled at his children. "Without me you'd all be nothings." They all sought approbation from the world, desperately wanting to be rich and famous to prove him wrong. Their mother looked outside, to speeches and international meetings to confer importance on herself, just as she now depended on the weather to please her husband, attempting to order a perfect day for him.

Leslie felt her stomach tighten, remembering the blow of her father's hand on the table, the might of it knocking over wineglasses, rivulets of burgundy blood seeping into the tablecloth; his fist, swollen and white with rage, shattering the front-porch door; his howling out the bedroom window into the coldest night of winter, threatening to jump if Jason did not return to college. He never laid a hand on his wife or children. Yet they all cowered from his cruel ragings, their mother trying to cradle the children while attempting to hold down his anger, wiping his sizzling brow until calm was restored to the house.

"The rain is supposed to continue all day," her mother persisted, running her index finger over the radio dial in search of a sunny forecast. "Your father works so hard. How could this happen to him?"

Their father did work so hard, and the slightest infraction by a child triggered a reminder from her. A bad report card. Missing your bedtime. Smoking pot. Making a phony phone call. Throwing away money that did not grow on trees, but seemed to cover all the charge accounts in town.

But how long, Leslie agonized, would they have to pay? He used money to thrash them into submission. What was this family holiday if not just another guilt trip, and Leslie cursed herself for going along with it one more time. "He's a bully," she shrieked. But no one seemed to hear the words, stuck in Leslie's throat.

"Let's have breakfast," Jason suggested. "There is nothing to be done about the rain."

Walking outside, Leslie saw that there was little hope for her mother on this day. The rain slashed her face like a volley of wet arrows, staining her cheeks with tears. A leaden sky looked as though it might entomb her for the rest of the holiday. "Leslie Rittman is reposing this week at Sandy Cove Hotel. . . . In lieu of flowers, please send contribution to the International Study Center for Domestic Violence, Peoria, Illinois." Her coffin could be housed in the rondavel that was always vacant. The blinds were, appropriately, drawn in that room, and Leslie would not mind the early morning shuffleboard games outside.

She might otherwise have found this scenario amusing, except for her increasingly frequent ruminations on suicide. The earth under her bare feet was damp and unfriendly, and she figured it must be soggier underground. Leslie Rittman decided that she preferred to die on a more clement day.

She had sounded out her parents recently about a mausoleum, which would eliminate the problem of worms and bacteria. The cost of buying and maintaining one, they argued, would eat up money Leslie might well live on. Besides, her parents had already reserved a family plot, just as they always booked a year or two in advance for rooms at Christmastime. They left no stones unturned. "You don't know how excruciating it is to look for a grave for someone," her father said. "Just be glad this is taken care of." Would he ever understand, Leslie wondered, about the agony of searching for a life she could call her own?

Back in her room Leslie busied herself with getting dressed, throwing on an outsized windbreaker she kept from her first sailing trip fifteen years ago. Jumping over puddles, she arrived at the dining room, now shielded from the rain by canvas flaps. The expressions on guests' faces looked as forlorn as the day. No doubt, when the rain let up they would sit on the beach and tilt their faces to the clouds.

"Why don't we go into town to shop?" Rebecca said over coffee, hoping to take her mother's mind off the weather.

Yes, dear, Leslie thought contemptuously, why don't you go shopping. You'll feel better. Wasn't a little nip into Saks the housewife's cocktail? But Sarah Rittman was no ordinary woman, except for the fact that she allowed her husband to make her feel this way. "Your mother has everything," he had said so often. "More clothes than she'll ever need, jewelry, status." And no Theodore. Or a Theodore who might well blow his stack when he saw what the weather was like on the island.

"One of you go to the desk and call Shinehead," her mother said, opening her bag. "Here, I have his number." At all times she kept her keys, money and credit cards on her. She also emptied the room of all her valuables and then double-locked the door. No matter that she knew all the maids and would have had to tip one of them to rob her.

While Leslie's father was unconcerned about possessions, he displayed a paranoia about the family's safety. Like some narcotics detective, he overhauled Leslie's first apartment in New York City before pronouncing it safe. Later, when she lived and worked in a two-story complex in Miami, her father complained that there was no doorman.

"There's no door," Leslie tried to explain. "How can you have a doorman without a door?"

To which he replied, "I don't care. You should have a doorman. I'll make the call and see that you have one."

In the town, smells of garlic, beer and sweat were suspended in the humid air. Coconut shells, soggy papers and crushed cigarettes floated in puddles of water from the rainstorm. Hating to shop, Leslie turned down her mother's offer of a dress and went instead to a damp fast-food place for a Pepsi. The rain left crystal drops on the windowpane. There was a telephone booth outside, and Leslie walked over to it, hesitating for a second. Then she dialed the operator.

"I hav to get the international operator, ma'am, just one second," the voice said. "What tis dah number?"

"Four one five, six five two, four seven five two." For an instant Leslie wanted to take it back. It reminded her of all the times she had stuck her hand in a mailbox to try to retrieve a letter she regretted writing.

"Okay, I hav her on the line now," the operator said. "She's trying to get your number."

The phone booth was hot and sticky, making Leslie perspire. She held her breath as the phone rang.

Click. No sound now.

Leslie pulled the receiver up and down on its hook, trying frantically to get the operator back.

"What tis dah problem, ma'am?" the first voice said. "We can't get tru."

"That's what I'd like to know," Leslie shouted. "What the hell is the problem?" She was screaming into the phone disc, demanding to know whether the call had gone through or Adam had just not answered, or hung up. Leslie needed some connection with her lover, prolonging it by hollering at the operator.

"Dah lines are busy right now," the operator said. "We can't get tru to dah States. Try bahk later, ma'am."

Relieved that the problem had to do with the phone system, Leslie walked back to the dress shop. Her mother was writing out checks for clothes that included campy workshirts with *Anlucia City Jail* and prison numbers printed on the back. The children loved silly presents. They all had shirts, like canvas sacks, with yellow birds embroidered on the pockets. Yet back home they disdained those polyester blouses with half the Golden Gate Bridge on the front and the rest on the back. Nor did they like to wear the New York skyline around their torsos.

Returning to the hotel, the family had lunch, one of the major activities of the day—which was beginning to seem interminable. Dinner was also an integral part of the program at the resort.

"The tuna-fish salad is excellent," Holly said. With little else to do on a rainy day on the island, people tended to regard the menu as a spicy novel, reading it over and over again.

Jason ordered a hamburger instead. He took a bite and then spit it into a napkin. "This is like dog meat."

"Try vomiting, Jason," Leslie snapped. "It will have the same effect on my stomach." Whenever anyone threw up or made a noise to that effect, Leslie followed suit automatically. One reason she had heretofore rejected motherhood was her intolerance of food dribbling out of a baby's mouth. She would rather play surrogate mother to a few kids she particularly liked. It was an ideal arrangement. She had all the pleasure of being around children without worrying about whether they brushed their teeth or did their homework.

A wave of nausea came over Leslie as she thought about her abortion three months before. She wiggled in her seat to detach her sweaty pants from the vinyl seat cushion. The elastic band on her cotton underpants was glued to her waist like the tape that fastened the gauze napkin around her pelvic region after the operation. Gobs of thick iron-dark blood, maybe a cell from the five-week-old fetus sucked out of Leslie's body, smeared the napkin, a grotesque finger painting, a Rorschach in red. She had not told Adam, and paid for the abortion herself. Otherwise he might have held her to the pregnancy, just as he placed his hand, like a beanie cap, over the top of her skull as he thrust his penis deep inside her. She had felt soiled from the operation. Rebecca came to visit, standing over the bed as if peering into a crib, and gave her colored lollipops with a rubber band around them. They pretended that Leslie had gone to the hospital to have her tonsils taken out. She could always count on Rebecca's collaboration on a fantasy.

The clouds were perilously black as they repaired to their rooms to read and await their father's arrival. There was concern that the plane might not land. Shinehead, having deposited them back at the hotel, was now posted at the airport, but unreachable because the phone lines were out all over the island.

An hour later a trim man with gray-flecked sandy hair around a bald spot walked hurriedly into the lobby. He wore a gray business suit and a tiny bow tie. His eyes were alert and intelligent, but for the moment he looked lost. A bellhop took his briefcase and carry-on suit bag out of his hand and directed him to the room.

"Oh, hello, dear." His wife beamed, holding his face in her hands and planting a kiss on his forehead.

"Some weather," he grumbled. "Where are all the children?"

"I'll get them while you change," she replied.

"Change into what?" he asked incredulously. "I'm certainly not going to put on bathing trunks in this weather."

Soon they gathered in his room. He cross-examined the children about their activities, and the holiday atmosphere became charged with the tension of his scrutiny.

"Jason," he carped, "that was some Godawful stock tip you gave me."

"Dad, I told you it was highly speculative."

"Never mind." His father shrugged. "You know I don't care about such things. In the course of my life what difference could it possibly make?"

"Then why did you mention it?"

His father looked beyond Jason's inquiry to ask how Holly was feeling.

"Fine, Judge Rittman," she said. Holly always addressed her father-in-law in this manner. Anything less formal he would consider rude.

Before the judgeship she called him *Mr.* Rittman. Leslie thought it was weird that few people ever called him by his first name, not even on the hotel tennis court with the pro saying, "Folks, I'd like you all to meet. This is Max and Jason and Norma and Jerry and Leslie and *Mr. Rittman* and Judy and Frank. . . ." Whatever the circumstance, he set the ground rules and everyone else played by them. He never worried about being different, because, as Theodore Rittman acknowledged himself, he was always right.

Rebecca told him about a man on her flight who kept sailing his yacht over to the beach to see her.

"Wait until he sees your meanness," her father chuckled, charmed by Rebecca's beauty and secure in the knowledge that she did not form attachments for too long.

He got up from a chair and rubbed Rebecca's head, pretending to pull her hair and affecting a mean expression to mimic her. "Do you talk to him in the same dulcet tones you use with your father?"

"Daddy," she pleaded, trying to pry his hand from her head, "stop it." She got away.

"Come over here, Rebecca," he begged. "Don't run away from your father."

Their mother interrupted, insisting that he rest before dinner.

"Here's an article that someone wrote on me," he said, ignoring his wife. "I had my secretary make copies."

He licked his finger to part the pages and handed a copy to each of them. It reminded Leslie of teachers passing out exams. They always seemed so stern. There was nothing easy about Theodore Rittman either.

"By the way, Leslie, I read one of your stories on the plane."

"Which one?"

"On the artist Robert Rauschenberg."

"Oh," she grunted. "It was ruined by the editor. He cut it to shreds for space reasons."

"Now you listen to me," he insisted. "It was a first-rate piece. It was compact and lively. You didn't use some of your fancy words that obscure ideas."

"Thanks." Leslie turned sullen.

"Now look," he continued, jabbing his finger at her. "I've read enough in my life to know what is good and what is not. This was an excellent story." Then, holding his jaw in his hands like someone with a toothache, he added, "But that magazine is really awful. Such junk they print."

It bothered Leslie that her father thought nothing of the magazine where she worked. At *You* she felt important, bounding up steps of airplanes that would take her in a single week to Miami, Atlanta and Los Angeles on stories. "Dr. Kissinger here," the deep throaty voice said over the phone. "Your letter was charming and witty, and I intended to respond sooner. But as you know, my good friend Nelson Rockefeller died, and I have been preparing the eulogy. If you are not past your deadline, would you like to come over to the apartment late this afternoon? How does five o'clock sound to you?"

One day Leslie would run into her father on the Washington shuttle. In her well-tailored pinstripe suit and with a handsome leather briefcase, she would board the plane and nonchalantly fold her coat on the overhead rack. "Leslie." And then she would look over her shoulder and see her father there. She would pull out dozens of clippings, spread them on the food tray and flip through them like a graduate of the Evelyn Woods speed-reading course. When the flight attendant came by with the ticket wagon, Leslie would casually hand over her credit card without looking up and distractedly sign her name on the receipt. Then, who should be walking up the aisle, stopping at her seat, putting his stubby hand, with the bitten fingernails, on her arm as a greeting? Henry Kissinger. She would introduce him to her father, who, once Kissinger was out of hearing range, would hiss, "He lied about Cambodia."

During a blizzard Leslie had been dispatched by an editor to the coldest point on Long Island, twenty miles away. Her father had been sufficiently impressed then. Returning to the office, she found a note stuck in her typewriter: "Daddy (sic) called and said that you are not to drive in this weather. He wants you to get a hotel room nearby and send the bill to his office." The P.S. read: "But you're allowed to build a snowman. Don't forget to put on your mittens."

"Theodore," her mother pleaded, "you've had no sleep."

"Okay, children," he sighed, "I'll see you later."

71

"There's a show tonight," their mother called out. "Everyone will be dressed."

"Who's everyone?" Leslie inquired facetiously.

"Everyone," she said resolutely.

Leslie tucked the article about her father in the pocket of her windbreaker to protect it from the rain. Back in the room she unfolded the pages and matted them down on the bed. Apparently the article had been written on Christmas day, when her father had stayed behind to finish up some work. She began reading:

• *Man-in-the-News:*

Judge Rittman, Legal Patriarch, Has an Enduring Track Record

By Roy Evans, Jr.

When Federal Court Judge Theodore Rittman was an attorney he arrived at work, seven days a week, at 7 AM and rarely quit before midnight, often stopping in Chicago, Boston and Los Angeles in the course of a single week.

The change from private practitioner to public servant has not slowed his rigorous pace. Since his appointment last year to the Federal Court, Eastern District, he continues to astound the legal community. At 64, Judge Rittman does not intend to alter his ways.

On Christmas, with the court in recess, he spent the day researching and writing decisions that his colleagues might have left alone until trials resume after the first of the year. In a Special Cardozo Lecture before the Association of the Bar of the City of New York, the judge, who rarely gives speeches or grants interviews, declared, "It is not right for defendants to languish in jails because of a backlog of cases from the previous year.

"I don't care whether the defendant is a poor black, a rich white parasite or an alleged member of the Mafia," he said.

"I make no judgments about these people. The only judgment I make is what the evidence at the trial permits me to find."

Judge Rittman, who was born in 1916 in Brooklyn, cannot remember a time when he did not want to be a lawyer. His professional interest was kindled by a maternal grandfather, a rabbi, for whom the Talmudic Commentaries by Rashi and Rambam proved that God was Justice. "For Judge Rittman," a law clerk commented, "Justice is God."

He worked during the day as a reader for a publishing house and attended Brooklyn Law School nights, forming an enduring habit of hard work and long hours. He started his own practice, handling a wide range of cases and earning millions of dollars over the years.

Yet as a high-powered attorney he would not hesitate to take on, free of charge, civil liberties cases, often involving student radicals denied the right to free speech.

"A real lawyer's lawyer," a former client and corporate chief proclaims. "He earned every cent, not by sitting on boards of companies he represented, but by sheer hard work. You could reach Ted at midnight in his office, and he would be as alert and attentive as if it were the middle of the afternoon."

Judge Rittman disdains a flabbiness of the body as much as of the mind. He thrives on work, requiring no more than five hours' sleep a night. He plays an occasional game of tennis. Whenever he can walk instead of ride in a car, he does.

For the last twenty-eight years he has lived in a stately old English Tudor home on Long Island's North Shore, with a swimming pool and tennis court in the backyard which he rarely finds time to use. The judge and his wife, a social worker and prominent lecturer, have been married more than forty years. They have two daughters, Leslie, 30, a journalist, and Rebecca, 28, a graphics artist; and a married son, Jason, 25, an investment analyst.

Judge Rittman, said to be able to recognize the opus number of most classical compositions and give detailed accounts of Civil War battles, often laces his legal writings with Shakespearean quotations.

When the judge joins his family shortly on their annual Caribbean holiday he plans to reread *Ulysses* and some pre-trial testimony for an upcoming case. He expects to fit this all into five days, the longest he ever spends on vacation.

Leslie could not help feeling proud of her father. Often her anger prevented her from experiencing the good parts of him. She read the article a few more times. One passage, about the grandfather, jumped off the page, demanding her attention. She remembered that this man was one of the few people about whom her father had ever spoken with deep respect and affection. "My grandfather was a beautiful man," her father had once told Leslie. "He came to live with us. He was smart and handsome. He was a rabbi. My mother did not care about anyone but him. She destroyed my father with her cruelty. My grandfather—her father—was all that mattered in her life. She was devoted to him one hundred percent."

Leslie was confused, dizzy from these convolutions. Where was her father, exactly, in all of this? Was he the grandfather? The mother? Or both? Leslie felt trapped somewhere inside this relationship. She sensed that she had already lived it, and knew she needed a fresh script for her own life. Her thoughts were too troubled for her to discuss them with Rebecca, who had just returned to the room to change for the evening.

"That was a terrific article on Daddy," Rebecca said cheerily.

"Yeah."

At dinner they both complimented their father on the story. Leslie gave her parents a belated present, an auto-graphed copy of Truman Capote's *A Christmas Memory*, inscribed by the author and with a list of amusing remem-brances of Christmases past on the island.

"Half dozen of one, six of another," Leslie joked as she handed them the book. It was a reference to Flo the Piano Player, long gone from the island. Flo knew clichés like the keyboard. One of her favorite lines was: "He looked like death itself," which nearly gave the Rittman family coronary failure from laughing so hard.

"Leslie, you have to sing "More" for us," Rebecca prodded. At ten Leslie was convinced that she was a chanteuse and got up on stage to sing that popular tune. Her voice was an unbroken, atonal waver. But it did not matter because no one could hear her above the loud laughter of the family.

"Stop it," Leslie begged. She was more upset about that single humiliation than about all the things she might have become, a tennis player, pianist, sportscaster, pediatrician, wife, mother.

"Come on Leslie, don't be a killjoy," Rebecca pressed. "If you sing 'More,' then Jason will do 'Kansas City.'" His rendition was a lot of screaming into the microphone and violent hip movement.

"I don't remember the words."

The fashion show was getting underway. Following each act Rebecca raced back to the room, changing into different outfits and walking onstage to the table as if part of the show.

"She's such an infant," her father said proudly.

Middle-aged couples were doing Arthur Murray dance steps to steel-band music. Rebecca grabbed Jason and they both ran out on the dance floor, where they performed extravagant dips and twirls and gave each other piggyback rides. Leslie laughed at their outrageous behavior, which seemed to ease her detachment from the hotel scene. Exhausted from playing, the children and their parents turned in early.

The rain had stopped and Leslie opened the door of her cottage to the sea. She could not sleep. The effect of the evening was somehow disquieting. For as long as her father bankrolled these trips, the children would be imprisoned in tropical playpens. Everyone in the family had been pegged into a hole since childhood, and climbing out of it would be no small feat. Often Leslie returned to the source of that gaping pain, comfortable and safe in its familiarity, in the hope of finding something that was maybe never there in the first place. Yet she needed to hold on to the innocence and purity of childhood and the privileged position of the clan, a comfortable overcoat in the bitter cold of winter, a romp on a Caribbean beach. She dug herself in deeper, catching her breath between bouts, the annual family holiday.

Rebecca was already fast asleep under the covers, having tucked herself in tightly. Leslie got out of bed and stood by the open door in the soft night air.

6

The sun burnished the window as Leslie watched her father underline legal briefs on the beach. Terrified that he might think she was fat, she tried on several swimsuits in front of the bathroom mirror. None of them seemed good enough. The one-piece, shrunk in the wash, hiked up to a fold of flesh just above the thigh. The form-fitter, while it ironed out any bulges, exposed too much cleavage. Her bikini showed a stomach slightly bloated with breakfast. She lifted the form-fitter off the floor and put a beach top over it. The bathroom got steamy, and she was eager to go for a swim. The door was stuck. With her full force she pushed it open.

Rebecca just managed to jump out of the way and avoid a black eye. "Damn it, you almost knocked me over!"

"Sorry."

"What were you doing in there all this time anyway?" Rebecca groused.

"The door was stuck. The bottom wasn't shaved enough."

"Then wait," Rebecca ordered, "until I put on my suit, in case I lock myself in."

They were always covering up in front of each other. The last time Leslie had seen her sister nude was the summer Rebecca was two and wobbling around the front lawn with her tushey in full view of the neighbors. On their mother's instructions none of the children were allowed to walk around the house, let alone their rooms, with no clothes on. She shut her eyes to the way their father skulked around his daughters' sexuality, grabbing them by the loops of their Levi's to draw them close, then sticking his hand down their underpants and squeezing their backsides. Somehow they managed to squirm out of his lap. About the time he stopped doing this, Leslie was told by her mother to ask his permission to wear a brassiere. Snorting with laughter, he advised her to buy a Band-Aid instead. Now both daughters were well-endowed, and he complained about their sister-in-law being "a flat-chested monkey."

"This shouldn't be your concern," Leslie dared to suggest. "She's Jason's wife."

"She's like a board," he sneered.

"So?"

"I don't see what Jason could possibly want with such a flat-chested girl."

End of discussion. But Leslie had a recurring dream in which she was making love to a woman. Suddenly this pair of hands, with her father's unmistakably wide thumbs, are covering the huge breasts, fondling them. There was no face or body, just hands, which stayed only a few seconds.

Rebecca kicked open the door, snapping Leslie to attention. "Let's go."

Leslie trailed her sister. This way she could hide her own

walk, like that of a lumbering high-school football player, which always seemed to require an apology. "I was a tomboy as a kid," Leslie would explain. The remark was more a defense than an accurate description of her body, perfectly proportioned, firm yet sensual, more so than her sister's. She inspected Rebecca from the back and spotted a cellulite pocket on her right thigh. Serves her right, Leslie gloated, for never moving her body except to wiggle her hips or twist her shoulder a certain way to turn men on.

On the beach her father held a legal envelope over his mouth as he conferred with her mother. No doubt it was a summit meeting on Leslie's posture. Though her father kept all sorts of confidentialities about court cases and former clients, he was incapable of holding back commentary on his own children, even in front of other people, friends and strangers alike.

He greeted Leslie, "You walk like a duck. It's very unattractive."

"It's my walk," Leslie said defiantly, knowing the moment she uttered the words that they made no sense.

Her mother tried to soften the effect of his criticism. "Leslie, try pointing both feet together."

Every holiday Leslie vowed that she would enroll in a posture school upon her return to the city. The idea seemed more appealing on the island, with native women balancing baskets of mangoes, oranges and bananas on their heads. But her determination faltered while she strutted in front of a mirror with a dictionary skidding over her Brillo head. The first time Leslie foolishly used the king-size annotated Webster's, on the theory it might restore her posture faster. Instead, her body folded under its weight like an accordion and she nearly dislocated her shoulder.

"We should have insisted you take a posture course," her mother reminded Leslie, "right after the back accident."

On a hot June afternoon her father had watched as a cousin of the children climbed to the top of the jungle gym in the backyard and stood there without holding on. Leslie then tried it with no hands. Falling through the metal bars, she bumped her head and back a few times as she plummeted to the ground. A week later she collapsed while jumping rope in the schoolyard. The nurse called Leslie's mother, who rushed her to the orthopedist. The diagnosis: a cracked vertebra and four broken ribs. That same morning Leslie was encased, from shoulder to pelvis, in a cast of plaster slathered over a cotton undershirt that later got itchy and scratchy. Dr. Linwood sucked on his pipe the whole time he was sculpting the cast. At school the kids followed Leslie into the bathroom to autograph her cast, drawing hearts, flowers and Cupid arrows on it. It got to be a ritual, with Leslie opening her blouse for friends to elaborate on these designs. By the end of the term there was scarcely any space left on the cast.

That summer had seemed peculiar to Leslie, with her mother off on a world tour and Rebecca away at day camp. Jason was only a baby, and Leslie played chopsticks on the piano with his nurse. Every night her father left fifty cents, a fortune for a seven-year-old girl, on her desk. Leslie bought baseball cards which she kept in a shoe box and occasionally splurged on a big puzzle or a lizard-skin autograph book.

The days passed until Friday afternoon when Nanny, her mother's mother, collected Leslie and took her on the train to her Brooklyn apartment. Leslie engulfed and smothered Nanny with kisses that were returned without equivocation. They would take the elevator to the fourth floor of her red-brick apartment building, turn left to the end of the hallway. At a small folding table covered with plaid plastic Leslie watched Nanny make potato latkes, her specialty. Overhead a miniature Swiss clock tick-tocked, and Leslie secretly wished she could hold back its hands forever. As soon as Leslie polished off her plate, more latkes would magically appear. "Enoof?" Nanny asked in her Yiddish accent. Nanny could replenish like nobody else. She then scooped up the potato skins from the wet counter and closed the can of chicken fat.

They always took a walk on the streets filled with the aroma of freshly baked bagels and knishes. It was Nanny's grandest pleasure to have Leslie around. "My grandchild Leslie," she announced to friends and strangers in the street. Leslie, wrapped in the folds of Nanny's cotton dress, faintly smelling of mothballs, waved hello. The two of them, Nanny and Leslie, were one, inviolate territory.

Leslie wouldn't let go long enough for Nanny to open her pocketbook and fetch a tiny black purse out of it. She had been a penniless Jewish immigrant, and she counted her change meticulously, out of habit. Nanny would have gladly emptied her pockets and piggy bank, sitting on the night table by the bed, for her grandchildren. In her will she bequeathed one thousand dollars to each of them. But Leslie could never bring herself to cash or deposit the check, and kept it hidden in a miniature jewelry box that resembled a Swiss chalet and played music when she opened its doors.

Leslie picked out comic books, which she was not allowed to read at home, a tin can of Pick Up Sticks, crayons and a coloring book. With the presents tucked in a brown bag under Nanny's arm, they wandered home, Nanny opening the door with a gold key on a piece of string. Leslie sat down on the Castro convertible, Nanny's prize possession, which would be opened later for her to sleep. As the afternoon wore on, with a sliver of sunlight receding behind olive-green felt curtains, she fell asleep in Nanny's arms. At five o'clock it was time to meet Papa, returning by subway from his job as a clothes cutter. He had made all the granddaughters black felt skirts with pink poodles on them. Leslie accompanied him to the allergy doctor for his weekly injection.

The weekend always seemed to be over too soon. "Next time," Leslie told Nanny, "I'm going to buy jars of glue, so then I won't be able to get up and we could stay here together all the time." Nanny laughed through her false teeth. Leslie was fascinated by the way she could remove them, and Nanny obliged with a demonstration. Then she talked without her teeth, now floating in pinkish water, and Leslie was so amused that she no longer felt so sad about leaving. Before getting on the train on Sunday afternoon, Nanny, a proud woman, put the false teeth back in her mouth—which was somehow never twisted with anger or contempt.

All the children loved Nanny for just plain being herself, this truly good person. She invested her life in Papa and after he died kept the company of his memory. Too shy to go to a resort, she wintered in New York rather than Miami. In her last years she became totally senile and incontinent, but never lost her physical strength, marching Leslie up and down the nursing home halls that reeked of mildewy, urine-soaked sheets. Whenever Leslie needed to feel good she thought of Nanny. A warm bath. A hot towel. A latke. There was no unfinished business, so she did not feel guilty or afraid about Nanny dying.

After the funeral they sat shivah, catered by a local restaurateur who brought two hundred bagels, cream cheese and lox, for a day. Leslie drove Nanny's nurse to the train station. Her name was Beulah, and she never minded that Nanny called her Faye. She had cared for Nanny like her own child, calming her with soft stroking of the hair and wiping the feces and urine leaking down Nanny's legs as though dabbing a baby with cotton puffs. Every morning she had arrived at the nursing home with an apple which she placed on the bed tray, cut in quarters and shared with Nanny. Beulah brought an apple to the funeral. Now she sat in the car revolving it in her hands. Then Beulah put the apple inside her pocketbook, opened the car door, walked with solemn dignity into the train station and disappeared.

As Leslie emerged from her memories she blurted out, "How come you didn't let me give the eulogy at Nanny's funeral?"

"Because it was stupid," Jason stated. "That part about Nanny being so worldly even though she never rode on a plane."

Mrs. Rittman hugged a straw pocketbook, filled with all her valuables, close to her chest and tapped on it. She wore a hat to shield herself from the sun that had put lovely wrinkles into Nanny's face. "You fictionalized it," she explained coolly. "Nanny went on the Boston shuttle to Aunt Mildred's son's Bar Mitzvah."

Behind her sunglasses Leslie squinted to trap the tears. But she could not hold back her anger, now realizing how tangled in her mind were Nanny's devotion and the abandonment by her mother she had felt that summer. "I would never put either of you in a nursing home," she shrieked.

"Please, Leslie, we'll discuss this later," her mother said, the set jaw twitching.

Leslie's father sprang out of his chair and into the sea, seemingly all in one motion. He wasted no time and did not suffer from indecision. Once, on the way to work, when he thought he might be suffering a heart attack, he told Clarence to stop at the doctor's office, which he visited every ten years. "Just pull over and wait," he instructed. "I'll be right out. I have people waiting in Washington for a meeting. I must make my flight."

He was in excellent health. Eliminating bread, potatoes and desserts from his diet, he had maintained the same weight, 160 pounds, for the last thirty years. He still fit into the bathing trunks bought five years ago by his wife, who did all his shopping. For tennis he used the same trunks, having no interest in designer sportswear. The only purchases he made for himself seemed to be books and classical music albums which arrived at the house in the mail. While it was his pleasure to shell out eight thousand dollars for a family holiday, he had a curious penury about himself. His bow ties cost two dollars—maybe five now, on account of inflation.

Jason swam out to meet him in the water.

"Oh, hello, son," he said, lifting his head out of the sea. In the last year or so he had started addressing Jason in this manner. Before that Jason might not have known where he stood with his father, who had taken him to a ball game only once, and then he had had to leave in the middle to go back to a meeting.

"Let's race," Jason challenged. "On your mark, get set . . . wait, I'm not ready. On your mark, get set, *go!*"

Almost immediately his father was out in front, plying the water in fast, even motions, never lifting his head to observe the competition. With his mind always racing ten steps ahead of most people, he automatically assumed that no one had the inside track on him. He walked out of the water and declared himself the winner with a huge grin.

"I'm sixty-four years old," he congratulated himself.

"Make sure you get your Medicaid forms," Sarah said playfully. "We'll be senior citizens next year."

"And don't forget the half-price bus card," Jason chuckled.

It was seldom that the family got a chance to be silly. Now their father's good mood gave them an opening to have a laugh, a recess from the tension. Abruptly, they stopped laughing.

He grimaced. "You don't think I'm going to stand on line like some moron to get those forms."

To bolster his youthful image Leslie's father often picked the most obscure historical question and challenged the children to answer it correctly. Then he waited about five seconds to give his reply: "I went to school forty years ago. It's amazing how I retain things. You're all out of school only a few years and don't remember anything. That's because you never learned anything."

Suddenly he was limping—over to the lounge chair, where he sat sideways and bent to inspect a tiny red mark, like that from an injection, on his foot. It got bigger and became a bump, swelling his whole foot.

"Sarah," he called out to his wife, now dunking her toes in the sea. "Come over here."

"What's wrong?"

"My foot is swollen."

"It must be a bug bite, dear."

The whole family gathered around their father to study the bite. They were joined by a peddler, a child whose arms were covered with scabs and beaded necklaces. She took a long look at his foot.

"Not-ting to it, mahn," the rascal, eager to make a sale, said. "It twill be gone soon. Here I have some tings to make you feel bettah."

Leslie, usually drawn to evil and mischievous children, shooed her away. She tended to panic about her father. Once when he sat at the dinner table, exhausted from an overseas flight, Leslie got scared when his head dropped— he was only picking a hair out of a bowl of soup. A thud from the basement boiler late at night caused her to fly down the stairs, post herself outside his bedroom and eavesdrop on his breathing. At such moments, a snore was a reassuring sound. "When I drop dead," her father joked, "I'll make sure the ambulance mutes the siren so you won't be frightened."

Frightened of what? Of seeing this man, who never stopped long enough for lunch, lying still in a coffin. At the funeral there would be competition among the children to keep their composure. But without him around to judge the winner, everyone might well fall apart and get hysterical, no longer having to prove anything to him. Now, while he was still alive, they sometimes speculated among themselves who would take it the worst and end up in a mental hospital.

Jason ran and got a doctor with whom he had played tennis earlier. It was clear from the man's lack of interest in the bump that he came from the medical school of "don't-call-me-on-Wednesday-I-have-a-golf-game." He lifted the foot in one hand and ran the fingers of his other over the huge red bump. Then he dropped the foot in the sand. He removed a pipe from the pocket of his candy-striped seersucker beach jacket, inserted it in his mouth and gave the diagnosis.

"You have a bite," the doctor said. "Are you allergic to penicillin?"

"No."

"Could you prescribe some?" Leslie asked impatiently.

"I don't have any prescription pads with me," he replied. "Otherwise I'd be making house calls around the cottages for swimmer's ear. Any doctor on the island can give you the pills."

Leslie ran to the front desk to fetch the house doctor, but was told he was on a boat trip and not expected until the evening. Picking up a local directory, she hurriedly thumbed through its damp yellow pages in search of a doctor. There were ten names in all. She dialed the first three without answer. The fourth picked up, and in a soft cultured accent told Leslie to meet him at the local hospital. There he would write out the prescription and fill it on the premises.

Back on the beach Leslie notified the family she was going for the pills.

"Now that's idiotic," her father said. "It can wait. You don't have to make a trip in this heat. Let Jason go."

"I have a sailing lesson in five minutes." He fidgeted. "But I'll cancel it."

"It's no trouble," Leslie pleaded. "I don't mind going."

Oblivious to her father's swollen foot, Rebecca held court on the beach for two teenage boys who could not do enough for her, running inside to get her a glass of water, making sure the suntan lotion covered every inch of her back.

"Let Leslie go," her mother said. "She wants to. Let her."

Her father pretended to hate anyone's fussing over him. He used to suffer from vicious migraines, but never asked the children to lower their Victrolas or stop bouncing a basketball against the wall. His pain had been blunted long ago by a mother who resented having to change the towels covering him during a long bout of rheumatic fever at the age of eighteen. "She did it out of duty," he recalled. "She was up all night, hating every minute of it. She couldn't even stand to touch the towels drenched with my sweat. She never complained aloud, but I remember how she would look away and hold her nose every time she had to touch the towel." When his mother died, he did not cry. Yet he had gone every morning and night for a month to the hospital where she lay in a coma after a stroke. Though the most successful of her children and the one who could send her to Miami and Israel, he had been the least favorite child. "But I respected her," he often snarled. "Every time my father said 'I'll do it tomorrow,' she would say, 'Tomorrow is coming. It always does.'" He loved his father, but disdained his lack of ambition and general irresponsibility, unable to forgive him for taking some of his older brother's college tuition money to buy season tickets to the opera.

Leslie grabbed the car keys and a towel to drape over the seat that absorbed the midday sun. Instinctively she opened the left door and then had to climb over the stick shift to the driver's seat on the right. It was one more incongruity on the island, driving on the left side of the road, British style, in a Japanese-made Toyota. A trade wind seemed to push the car down a steep hill. Leslie always experienced a shortness of breath at such a loss of control. Though agile in sports, she was inept with an automobile and a moron with directions. Unless someone specifically told her about turning right at the school and then hanging a left at the firehouse, she could not find her way. She loved the way other people read maps, spreading them over the steering wheel and running a finger over a highway. The light tapping sound pleased her. Folding the map was like trying to do a jigsaw puzzle, and she could never get the flaps to fall into place.

She kept her eyes fixed on the carbuncular road. Up ahead, the frescoed pink and lime homes with their red-tiled roofs looked scrubbed and bleached. Underwear flapped in the wind outside native huts. A Volkswagen bus ferrying workers to their jobs whizzed by, hurling pebbles against her windshield. She mashed the gas pedal, braking only around precarious bends in the road, honking at a teenage boy veering toward the middle of the road on a delapidated Moped.

Leslie had always meant to tour the island, but never did, regretting this whenever she boarded the plane to return home. On her one brief foray, mammoth bats chased her out of a limestone cave. She was curious, though, about the rain forest, with a plant that shriveled from the touch of a human hand. Leslie backed off, too, from such contact, shrinking from the proffered kisses and hugs of acquaintances on the street or at parties. These emotional withdrawals sometimes made her lonely for a pat on the back, and then she went to the beauty parlor for a shampoo, to feel someone's anonymous hands rubbing her head, all she could manage then.

The island hospital was just ahead on the right side of the road. It was a one-story pastel pink building on a patch of dirt, with one palm tree scratching the side window. There was no door, only an archway. Inside, a mother sat on a folding chair with two small children crawling all over her. The linoleum floor, still damp from a scrubbing, smelled of ammonia. A flimsy curtain was drawn over what appeared to be the examining room.

"Is anyone here?" Leslie called out.

The mother stared at the curtain. She sat with her legs apart and slapped her feet against the soles of her rubber thongs.

Either no one got sick on the island or everyone had been killed off by inattention. Twenty minutes passed before a nurse appeared, ushered the mother and children past the curtain and quickly closed it. Seeing that it was impossible to knock on a curtain, Leslie sat and fumed. In most hospitals—and this one was no different—the seats were arranged so that no one should step out of line. The only way to get attention, Leslie figured, was to drop dead on the spot. By then, of course, it was too late. Usually the biggest noisemaker got seen by a doctor first. The order made no sense. Stroke victims were not known for hollering at some two-finger typist at an admitting desk.

The nurse drew open the curtain and popped her head out. "Yes, ma'am?"

"My name is Rittman, and I'm supposed to meet Dr. Anduze here."

"He be bahk."

"When?"

"Who could say. . . . Tings come up, emergencies."

Leslie was starting to feel sick with worry about getting the pills to rescue her father. Was she doing him a favor? Or just being an obedient daughter? Whatever, she felt as if she were late meeting him at a restaurant, fearful that he would holler at her. Now she worried about her mother, who must be wondering whether Leslie had been mugged in broad daylight or had just run off the road into a ravine. She picked a cobweb out of the pay phone and dialed the hotel. The phone was dead. She slammed the receiver against the box, trying to shake a sound out of it. Just as she felt the power going out of her body, she sat down. Leslie thought she would pass out, but concentrated on restoring her balance by calling upon her father's words: "We are not a fainting family."

Two hours later a tall, thin man in a white doctor's coat entered the hospital. His golden-brown skin had an Oriental tone and his large black eyes flashed a quick intelligence. "Are you Miss Rittman? I'm sorry for the delay, but I had an emergency at one of the hotels. Come with me."

He led her down a narrow hallway into a room no larger than a closet. Two microscopes sat on a concrete counter with slides, like dirty dishes around a sink. Under the counter were huge wooden drawers. He opened one of them and pulled out packages of envelopes with pills inside them. Typed on the outside was *Penicillin, 500 milligrams.* He stuffed ten packages in her hands. "You have enough pills here for ten days, four times a day."

"How much do I owe you?"

"Don't bother about it," Dr. Anduze said, softly patting her hand. "We have plenty more here. And I kept you waiting a long time."

His calm, generous manner diffused her irritation at the long wait, and her mood was such at this moment that she did not care to argue with him about a bill. She thanked him and ran to the car. Putting the pills in the cool, dark glove compartment, she turned the key of the car and took off at breakneck speed for the hotel.

Leslie tapped on the door of her parents' cottage, then saw that her mother was chatting with another woman on the patio. Leslie recognized her as Carla Baker, a New York politician.

"Good," Sarah said. "I'm glad you're back. What took so long? I was worried something might have happened. Your father is napping." Then, turning to her guest, she added, "This is my daughter Leslie."

Leslie acknowledged the introduction with a nod. "The doctor kept me waiting," she said. "He said he had an emergency. How's Daddy's foot?"

"Still swollen, but I'm going to wake him for his pill."

"Okay, see you at dinner."

"Thanks, Leslie."

"Sure."

It was after four. The interval between late afternoon and dinner was always torturous for Leslie. On the island the passage of time was as imperceptible as the change of seasons. Drowsy from the sun she had gotten in the morning, yet not tired enough to sleep, Leslie fidgeted inside her room. It was loneliness that made her so uncomfortable with herself. She lay on the bed and stretched out her arm as if reaching for Adam's hand. Her arm felt like an appendage that did not belong to her, stranded on the bed. Rebecca was not back yet. At least she might have filled the room with her chatter.

She heard footsteps, a slow shuffle, probably a waiter pausing outside someone's door with a tray of cocktails and cheeses balanced on his palm. There were precise rhythms, the pitter-patter of barefoot children, the sandpaper scraping of ancient couples or the sprightly step of the suburban housewife in her espadrilles. Everyone thought someone else was going somewhere, when actually nobody was going anywhere. Where did they all think they were going? To breakfast? Lunch? Dinner? At least there was comfort in a shared journey nowhere. At night their shadows came in pairs, two etchings moving in the dark.

Leslie had tried to synchronize her motions with Adam's, but ended up resenting him for it. Sometimes, as much as she longed to be with him, she would be late, a gesture of arrogance on her part. She was always two steps ahead of him at a gallery opening, buying her own program which made Adam feel she was somehow taking something away from him. Her drive for money was enormous, but she wanted it on her own terms, not as a derivation of someone else, a husband or parents.

As Leslie dressed for dinner, in tailored beige pants and an expensive cotton blouse, she wondered at what moment she had stopped feeling like wearing cool, backless dresses. Her smooth skin was baby-soft and richly tan, and yet she felt a need to cover it up. Leslie hid from herself. She worried that soon she would be old and was wasting her body. Of late Leslie had started putting her hands in her pants pockets, detracting still more from her femininity. It was like chain-smoking when she was trying to recover from a chest cold.

"Stand up straight," Rebecca commanded as she glided into the room. Honest to the point of being blunt in all areas of her life, she was the kind of person who really studied someone and told her how she looked. Rebecca pulled a halter dress off a hanger and wrapped it around her thin body. No matter what she put on, she looked terrific. She could eat french fries, two Milky Ways, drink six Pepsi-Colas a day and never gain a pound. She loved to shop and dress up, a reaction perhaps to the hand-me-downs she got as the baby sister. She handled clothes with ease, draping them over chairs in a relaxed fashion.

Leslie often left her best dresses behind because they were too good to pack. The outfits stayed, like spinsters in an attic, neatly put away.

"What are you saving the clothes for?" her mother often inquired amusedly.

Leslie explained, "I don't want to wear them out."

That, her mother said, was silly. "Clothes are supposed to be worn. That's what they're for."

Life was supposed to be lived; that's what it was for, right? Leslie was saving up for a time when she would be free of the family, completely on her own, wealthy enough to walk away. How could it be that she lived for thirty years with this family and no one knew her? Then suddenly there would be this stranger who understood without Leslie saying one word. But that immediate understanding might change who she was, and it frightened her.

"Tell Mommy I'll be there in a minute," Rebecca called out as Leslie left the cottage.

Everyone was on the terrace having cocktails, the pinkish rum concoctions blending in with the freshly picked yellow and white roses arranged in an ivory vase.

"Where's Rebecca," her mother said. "Why can't she be on time like everyone else?"

"She'll be here momentarily," Leslie said, glad of this pause, leisurely and tropical, but not for long.

"We're not going to wait for her any longer," her mother snapped. "One day she'll find herself with no one around."

"Stop it, dear," her husband shot back. "Why do you have such a lack of patience with her? I hear the way you talk to her."

"That's your fantasy." She sulked.

He shook his head to show disappointment at his wife's behavior and in the hope of making her feel guilty and ashamed about it. "She's like an infant," he cooed, "and she's never going to change. She needs us."

He kept Rebecca that way, out of his need to know there was one child unable to find her own way. Often Rebecca delayed any action in her life while he untangled a predicament for her, usually compounding it. A part of him did not want her to succeed, in order that she remain dependent on him.

A huge grin spread over his face as Rebecca made her entrance onto the terrace. "Here she is now." He beamed, rising from his chair to greet and pull her toward him.

"Let's go," his wife grumped. "Everyone is hungry."

"Wait," Rebecca snapped. "I want to have a drink before dinner."

"Hold on," her father said, waving his hands in front of their faces as if they were in monkey cages. "Why are you all in such a hurry? It's not the Last Supper."

Leslie hated to have supper with him anywhere. He wound up all the waiters in the place, shouting at them, stepping on them like ants. Then he changed his table because someone next to him was smoking a cigar or shoveling food into his mouth. Guilt-ridden, he handed out tips like play money, spreading it around quietly, tucking the bills in a captain's jacket, folding them in a waiter's hand, but always making eye contact—menacing glances, lest anyone forget his generosity. He paid these people off, just like his children, to be obedient. No one ever talked back to him, but their sighs of relief descended on the room as he left it.

"Your table is ready, sir," said a friendly-faced islander in a shimmering black tuxedo with a royal blue cummerbund around his tiny waist.

As her father got up from the table Leslie saw that he was wearing a sneaker with the top flap cut out to accommodate the swollen foot. He limped slightly, but refused to acknowledge any pain.

"How is his foot?" she whispered.

"A little better," her mother said. "Thanks for getting the pills."

Her father ordered a double Canadian on the rocks.

"You can't drink with the pills," her mother warned.

"It's all right," he mumbled. "It can't hurt."

He had the most extraordinary recuperative powers. On the way to work one Sunday, the only day he drove himself, he rammed into a telephone pole while reading a law article. Untangling the grille of the car, he drove back home with a bump on his forehead and three broken ribs. He mentioned the accident to his wife in the same voice he might have used to report a flat tire, and then drove her car to the city. Pumping himself with aspirin, he put in ten hours at the office. Two days later he seemed fully recovered. Sometimes Leslie thought he possessed superhuman powers, the bionic judge.

The wine steward arrived at the table and held open the list. "Will it be red or white tonight?"

It was like color war at the table with half the family lining up with the reds and the other behind the whites. Eventually they agreed on the two kinds.

Always her father started off the dinner on a pleasant note: The President is inept, or there's a depression around the corner, or a writer, all dried up, finished, hasn't written anything decent in ten years. Leslie imagined him hunched over a paper, scrutinizing it for the most misanthropic news of the day to repeat at meals. As children they had felt tense when they heard his footsteps in the house. "Who's going to get it tonight?" Now he picked on the President, and they were relieved.

His tirades, even directed against someone other than herself, bombarded Leslie. She took them all in, and then did not know how to let them out, as if she were choking on a mouthful of air sucked into her lungs. She searched for a defense even before the attack was made. Now she was full of pain from his having overlooked her good deed in getting the pills.

She drank her wine in hurried gulps, to make the dinner a blur. Over the years Leslie learned to tune him out, by controlled reverie, looking interested without listening to one word. Conversations became a distant drone, warplanes zooming overhead in a jungle.

"Leslie," Jason reprimanded, "don't chug-a-lug the wine."

"I know how to drink wine."

"Well, you're not doing a very good job of it."

"Don't be such an expert on everything," Leslie said.

Her father interrupted, wanting to know what the argument was about.

"He's just a big arrogant kid," Leslie said. "A know-it-all."

"Stop it," he growled. "You have to be a moron to get into an argument with him. You're supposed to be an adult and you get involved in a silly argument with a little boy."

"I'm not a little boy," Jason wailed.

"He certainly isn't," her father said, adding, "Don't you be so resentful of him. If you had a man in your life, then you wouldn't be so grumpy."

"Your faddah says you need a good fuck," the shrink had told her. "Dat's vat your faddah says." Ten years before, she had met Dr. Sandor Meyer at her parents' party and told him she had problems with relationships. "I probably shouldn't bother you with this now," Leslie apologized. "I suppose it's like asking an internist to look at my throat." He told her to call and make an appointment. She rang him up and over the course of the few months that she saw him, Dr. Meyer was to get a look at a lot more than Leslie's throat. "A faddah fixation," he told her while shoving his penis inside her on the couch. "Dat's vat you haf." When she quit therapy with him Dr. Meyer told her something even more original: "Dis is de first time I do dis vit my patient."

Now, Leslie tried to find an answer for her father. His face was red hot, burning with contempt. Shaking, she did not know if the tremors came from fear or rage inside herself. Her unspoken words choked her and left her speechless.

Exhausted by her unsuccessful effort to win this battle with her father, Leslie turned inward. She was dimly aware that they were joined at one point by Rebecca's date. He wore a custom-made French shirt with a monogram and soft leather shoes with no socks. He had the look of success, probably jogged every morning and did not smoke cigarettes.

"Sit down," her father said. "Would you like something to eat?"

Seeing that the plates were being cleared from the table, he declined the offer of food.

"My name is Mark," he said. "Pleased to meet you, sir."

"Have some dessert," her father said, possessively combing Rebecca's hair with his fingers.

"No thanks," Mark replied. He looked at his watch and at Rebecca. "We're running a little late."

"Just sit," her father ordered him. "You don't have to run. Whatever it is, it will wait."

Adam had resented the way Leslie's father talked to him and told her so. At dinner her father had grilled Adam, forty years old, about his college major, Cavalier poets, English literature. Leslie loved it that Adam talked back. "Why is this important?" he demanded to know. "I am sure, sir, that you might find it more interesting to talk about paintings, something I do now, than having me dredge up a poem I read twenty years ago." He had pressed Leslie's hand under the table as her father hurled an unpleasantry at her about a pimple on her face. With the meal over, Adam, his hands gently massaging her shoulders as he followed her into the den, whispered urgently, "Let's get out of here. Haven't you had enough of this crap? Are you some sort of masochist?" Now without him she felt defenseless, with Mark fidgeting at the table, Rebecca playing him off against her father, and Jason nuzzling Holly.

Isolated in her despair, Leslie said she had a stomach ache and asked to be excused from the table.

"Where are you running?" her father challenged.

"I'm not feeling well. My stomach hurts."

"Sit here and have some tea now."

"Let her go," Leslie's mother intervened.

Inside the cottage the tears felt like hot marbles running over her face. She tried to sleep, but was still awake after three hours. Leslie got up, dressed and walked out the door. The full moon was sliced up by the fronds of a palm tree in her view. The hotel was empty of people, quiet. A wrought-iron gate prevented her from passing through the lobby. She heard the lackadaisical steps of the night guard at the end of the pathway. Walking around the back of the cottages, she saw that the car was gone and looked for a taxi to take her to the casino.

Leslie waited there, alone, in the driveway.

7

The calypso pace of the island picked up in the casino,
and Leslie felt a rush in her head from the flash and ring of
slot machines, the clatter of chips and the shuffle of cards
through hands decorated with flashy bracelets and diamond
rings. The thick rust carpet felt like air under her feet as she
walked over to a blackjack table to watch a hand. She recognized a man from the hotel sitting in the fifth seat around
the horseshoe-shaped table. He was said to have the Midas
touch, but now he was nervously counting three remaining
hundred-dollar chips, bouncing them on the palm of his
hand. Earlier in the day Leslie had observed him on the
beach, flicking tiny bubbles of salt water off his skin and
then patting the hairs on his arms in an even direction. She
surveyed the place, looking for other guests from Sandy
Cove, and saw that the head count was limited to herself
and the luckless Midas.

Two fair-skinned preppies wearing seersucker jackets

and Weejuns without socks walked around the casino with dollar chips as though they were playing Skee-Ball at an amusement park. They appeared to be sensible young men who would rather spend their money on a sailboat rental than a roller-coaster ride at the tables. Leslie identified more with them than with the other habitués of the casino. They spoke in quiet snickers, in sharp contrast to the orgasmic grunts coming from the crap table at the far end of the gold-chandeliered room.

Leslie wobbled through the casino to the seedy elegance of its Italian restaurant with gushing fountains and sugary Jimmy Rosselli piped into the sound system. She sat down at a Formica-topped counter and shivered from the damn air conditioning while hot flashes struck her body like lightning. The place was the taxi drivers' local diner. Every couple of hours they scouted the casino for their passengers, standing unobtrusively in full view without disturbing their concentration. Usually gamblers had the drivers wait because "we'll only be an hour or two," which more often than not stretched out into an all-night vigil. Leslie ordered a Pepsi-Cola, which she drank through a red and white pinstripe straw.

There was a light poke in the middle of her back and then, "Would dah lovely lady like to go down to deh town to dance?"

Looking up from her glass, Leslie saw standing over her a lanky black boy, no older than sixteen and wearing tight, shiny black waiter's trousers. His hands were crisscrossed and locked behind his back as he strutted in place.

"No, thanks," she said, vaguely amused by his gall. At least the boy did not have the oleaginous charm of leisure-suited salesmen who approached her in hotel bars when she occasionally stopped for a drink on a business trip. In recent times, however, she had preferred to order from room service rather than suffer through a set of Barry Manilow songs performed by some urban hillbilly in the cocktail lounge.

"Okay, mahn," the boy said sheepishly, darting out of her way on the heels of his black basketball sneakers.

Why couldn't people, Leslie wondered, leave her alone with her thoughts? Whenever she traveled abroad she enjoyed sitting at a café, reading a newspaper and writing letters. Without fail a strange man would stop by her table and remark, "Quelle tristesse." She looked through the air at his overture while assuring him that there was nothing particularly "triste" about her. Even when reality, the presence of an attractive suitor, treated Leslie well, she needed to hold on to a fantasy. "Wake up," Adam told her often. "You're someplace else." It was hard to sustain anyone else's presence for long. Sometimes when the two of them lay on the bed a heaviness seemed to strap her to it and she felt herself sinking into the floor. Since her father's arrival on the island Leslie had felt the weight of his rejection.

She twirled the straw, creating foamy bubbles in the soft drink. Everything tasted better through a straw, except the yellowish bent ones that came with hospital meals. In fourth-grade dance class the greenish cafeteria walls, with the folding chairs pushed against them, had closed in on Leslie when she caught her boyfriend and best friend Babs Edelman sharing a container of chocolate milk through a straw. Seeing Leslie's pain, Babs pushed the straw away and instantly broke off the romance. Though Leslie had not seen her since high school, whenever the name Babs Edelman came up in conversation with some longtime chums she blurted out, "Babs is one of the most loyal friends a person could have."

It had been a long time since Leslie trusted anyone. Though she attracted accomplished and good-looking people, she had too often been sucked in by sycophants whose flatteries were veiled hostilities and jealousies. For the price of a compliment she had allowed them to trespass on her life.

If Leslie could hit the jackpot she would build a wall to keep the shit out. It would be so high that she would not be able to peer over it and get a whiff of the odor. Inside her immaculate white palace grounds she would have a tennis court and serve lemonade between sets out of chilled empty ball cans with matching straws. Her guests, all trim and fit from the active sporting life, would wear simple running shorts and T-shirts. Jasmine vines would tickle the house and creep through the large picture window in the breakfast room, filling the whole place with their delicious scent. Blushes of blue sky would push all the clouds away, and the sun would dapple the green leaves with golden hues. Every day would be sunny and happy.

Leslie walked out into the dim lights that collected gray swirls of cigar smoke. Round heavy glass ashtrays over-flowed with cigarettes. Melted ice water that collected ashes dribbled all over brown bar trays holding plastic cups, with lemon and lime twists perched atop mixers shaped like palm trees. She wondered what a goody-goody health nut like herself was doing in such a place. In Leslie's sopho-more year of high school her mother had gone on a radio program about teenage drug users and admitted publicly that all her children, except Leslie, had tried pot. During the commercial break Leslie plugged into the show with an emergency call to her mother. "I smoked pot, Mom," she pleaded. "I swear I did. If you don't go back on and say so I'll lose all my friends." Saturdays, when the children were rounded up in the back of the limousine bound for a museum or Broadway matinee, Leslie peered out the win-dow at some hood, with his duck cut and leather jacket, and wished she could knock around like that.

She went over to the cash window and slipped a two-thousand-dollar check through the metal bars. The woman inside swiveled around on a stool to talk to someone in an adjoining office. Moments later a jock type, a little over six feet with blond good looks, the kind that would fall apart in his mid-forties from too much booze, came outside. He uncreased the check and stared at the name on it.

"Aren't you the judge's daughter?"

"Yes."

He guided Leslie over to the cage and handed the check back to the cashier. "It's okay," he said. "I know the family."

On her infrequent gambling forays, Leslie's mother often had the children in tow, giving each of them a fistful of dollar chips and filling up paper cups with quarters for the slot machines lined up like so many gravestones. Guilt-ridden about denying her brood anything, she sometimes could not discriminate between what was good for them and what was bad. She bought cartons of cigarettes if anyone ran out of a pack. If one of her children was on a diet and eyeing a piece of cake, she offered kindly, "Have some cake. It won't hurt you. Here, I'll cut a small piece." Though she knew Leslie played the lottery and collected gas station coupons she would say, "Your father has to give a speech in Las Vegas this weekend. Why don't you come along?"

Leslie's mother rarely gambled more than twenty dollars a night and usually walked away breaking even or slightly ahead. Though she had lavish spending habits with regard to the children, dinners, trips and clothes, she was never reckless with money. An occasional excess had to do instead with opening a savings account at a new branch bank giving away free radios or buying a case of blinding orange tennis balls on sale. A high-rolling Arab sheik she was not. Yet her huge diamond ring with the rainbow light refractions had not gone unnoticed in the casino.

The manager delivered a yellow receipt to the dealer at

the blackjack table where Leslie took the only vacant seat, second from the far right. The man next to her had flecks of dry skin on his face and curled his index finger like an arthritic to call for a card. On her left a blond housewife carefully lifted each chip to preserve her freshly painted red nail polish. Her golden-haired daughter reached into her mother's bank of chips to double a dollar bet. At the far left, a fortyish man in a light blue monogrammed shirt and yellow linen jacket held his sunburned, sagging face in his hands as though he had a migraine.

"How do you want it?" the dealer asked Leslie. Coolly courteous, he spoke in a soft voice. But his huge black hands, glittering with diamond-studded rings and a thick gold ID bracelet, were rarely quiet.

"In twenty-five-dollar chips," Leslie replied. The casino manager, lightly pinching the dealer's elbow, left the area.

Without blinking an eye the dealer made two tall stacks of green chips, instantly paring them down to eight piles and sliding them in her direction. Leslie was mesmerized by his smooth, seemingly effortless motions, the tidiness of them.

The dealer placed the cards soundlessly on the green felt table and handed Leslie a joker to cut the deck. Then, scooping up the cards, he shoved them into a shiny brown canister, picking up speed as he dealt the first hand. Quickly Leslie pushed two twenty-five-dollar chips into the betting area and won. She doubled up for a hundred-dollar bet and beat him again. Now ahead one hundred and fifty dollars she started another hundred-dollar pile of four chips and put the extra two next to it. Pulling back, she picked one chip up and put it out, scoring, and then took one off for another single bet, for still another winner. Next she lined up the two hundred-dollar piles and then played half for a blackjack that put her winnings up to 350 dollars. The hot stares from her co-players turned now into cool, admiring glances, as Leslie buried her original two-thousand-dollar investment in her pocketbook. The housewife on her left smiled approvingly, as though Leslie were a good little girl for putting the money safely in a savings account.

Most of her life Leslie had banked on the elusive family trust fund that kept her tottering as she was now doing in the casino. "Why are you so frantic about making money when you have a measure of financial independence?" her father had often scolded, announcing in the next breath, "When I die, there will be nothing left. All finished. The money will have no value." The call would come late at night saying that her father had dropped dead over the law books in his chambers. None of the children would have enough savings, having spent their salaries on trips and other whims, to afford his funeral. Determined that no such burden should fall on her mother, Leslie would manage to come up with the ready cash to finance this last and well-deserved rest.

Now she took four chips from her winnings and got two queens. Splitting them, she laid another hundred-dollars-worth of chips on the table. The dealer had a king showing and threw her a two for a grand total of twelve on the one hand. Hit. Out came a ten and she was over. Then came another ten for the other hand to make twenty. Finally, the dealer pulled a nine, stopping at nineteen. Winning one hand and losing the other, Leslie was even, bailed out again—like the way dividend checks arrived in the mail to preserve a bank balance after a spending spree.

Leslie was dizzy from the ups and downs of gambling. She plunked down all her winnings on one hand, and lost. She pulled chips out of her bag, dumping them on the table in sloppy piles, some of them spilling into the betting box. As a little girl she had been frightened of the seesaw in the backyard, the way it climbed so quickly and plummeted the next second. She had never learned to balance herself on the treacherous toy. As fast as she sprayed the table with chips they vanished with the flicker of the dealer's hand. Reaching deep inside her pocketbook again, Leslie frantically brushed the bottom and sides to sweep out more chips. She touched one chip with the tip of her index finger, but it slipped out of her wet hand. Grabbing hold of it she tossed her last twenty-five-dollar chip on the table. The dealer had a king showing, and Leslie drew two cards for a lowly twelve. He paused while she held her breath. Encouraged by his raised eyebrow, she called for another card. Slowly, torturously, he flipped over her next card, letting it sail through the air, then crash down on her. A ten, and she was over twenty-one. Bust.

Stunned, Leslie raced frantically to the cashier and asked for the casino manager, who appeared before she finished her sentence.

"I'd like another thousand," she said.

"Can you cover it?"

"I have the money," Leslie said, her eyes fixed on the floor. "But I don't have any checks on me. I'll send it as soon as I return."

"When will that be?"

"In a day or two," Leslie pleaded. "I'll wire it."

"Okay," the casino manager said.

Her life was a series of reprieves that required adjustments in her game plan. Always, Leslie set enormous goals for herself and often felt paralyzed by the pressure of meeting them. Instead of now trying to break the house, she would concentrate solely on retrieving the two thousand dollars and then clearing another five hundred to fly to California to be with Adam. Total financial independence from the family would have to come at a later visit to a casino. "These prices are incredible," her father declared at a New York restaurant. "But have whatever you like." Though he never quibbled over or scrutinized a tab, he still needed to display the potency of his purchasing power.

Unless he spoon-fed his children luxuries, he was resentful of their tasting them on their own.

The first time she spent money without experiencing a tightness in her stomach was after receiving a huge book-royalty check, quickly consumed by bills for hotel suites stocked with champagne and caviar, hundred-dollar dinners and weekend jaunts south to play tennis in winter. But even when Leslie was poor, she lived well. Without fail her mother reminded Leslie, "Without the money you get from us you could not make all those trips," as though Leslie had never put in all those fifteen-hour days at her office. Her parents' largesse was a curious incarnation of stinginess which Leslie tried to shake off in various ways. At the time of her windfall Leslie had given a fifteen-year-old surrogate son and pal a Victrola to put in his boarding school room. "If you thank me one more time," she warned, "you will destroy the pleasure of giving you something nice. You must never mention it."

Back at the table, the washed-out man on her right wished her luck, while the housewife poked her daughter to take note that the degenerate gambler was back in the game. The dealers had already rotated and another black man took over, his expansive chest dominating the table. The light from the chandelier bounced off his shiny, co-logned bald head framed by Dumbo ears. Having received a yellow receipt from the casino manager, he shoveled chips in front of Leslie and then distributed the second card to each of the players. She put down five hundred dollars worth of chips on the next hand, on the theory that a few winners in a row would do the trick, quickly and painlessly. Then she would get up instead of getting greedy. The dealer had an ace showing. Leslie stuck at nineteen.

"Insurance," the dealer offered. The word was both a question and a rhetorical statement.

The housewife was confused now. "Insurance?" she

blurted out. "What is this? Isn't it enough they take your money? Now they're selling premiums?"

The dealer impatiently picked a half-dollar chip off her pile and stuck it in front of the dollar chip in her betting box. "If you want to protect your bet," he explained distantly, "then you keep this here in case I get a blackjack. Half your bet down protects your hand."

Her incomprehension drew exasperated grunts from the other players. The dealer teased her, spinning the chip on its side as he awaited a reply. The woman grabbed the chip and put it back in her pile.

By then the dealer's attention focused on Leslie, who lifted 250 in chips to protect her bet. Then she gingerly took them back.

"You don't want insurance?" the dealer inquired with a hint of intimacy, broken by a subtle sigh of impatience.

Leslie's hand jerked as she picked up the "insurance" again and put it back, then pulled back, finally leaving it there. The dealer's lowered eyes seemed to glue the chips to the table, making up her mind. Lifting his card, he held it close to his eyes and then, expressionless, let it drop on the ace. A nine. Twenty. Bust. Leslie was out another 750.

She could not concentrate through the haze of smoke from the cigarettes she was chain-smoking, courtesy of the casino. With the 250 dollars in chips remaining, it would take too long to win on conservative bets, she figured, and plunked down the whole sum. If Leslie was fuzzy about the arithmetic, the housewife kept an exact tally of the cash outflow. Leslie glared at her as the dealer made up another shoe. It seemed to take forever. She pulled a six and then a ten, sticking because the dealer had a two showing. Then he dealt himself a ten followed by a nine that gave him exactly twenty-one. Leslie moaned as he swooped up all her chips.

Now the casino manager was standing in the pit, and she

signaled him with two fingers, indicating another two grand. Magically, the chips appeared. The housewife and her daughter got up from the table as though offended by a porno movie. Leslie spread her bets, a thousand each, to play two hands. She drew an eighteen and a nineteen to the dealer's king. The sunburned man, now in a gray stupor, vacillated about whether to hit on thirteen. Under the leather-stuffed ledge of the table Leslie crossed her fingers for him to stick. He called for a card, and she cursed him under her breath. A six, giving him nineteen but increasing the dealers's chance to beat everyone with a color card, a queen, twenty. Bust, again.

Running from the table, Leslie crouched, as though she had to urinate, in the middle of the casino. Taut and immobile, like someone with a yellowjacket buzzing around, she tried to gain control of herself, to make some decision about her next move. Five thousand down the drain. It could be worse. Why not better? So many times she had walked out of her apartment depressed and then, seeing a crippled or deformed person on the street, suddenly felt better about her own life. Just as Leslie lost track of the casino chips, she could not reckon with her own worth.

She looked up to find the casino manager beside her, his sharp blue eyes fixed on her, feigning concern. "Are you okay?"

"Yes," she said, trying to swallow with a dry throat. Remembering the confidence she summoned to get her magazine interviews, Leslie used the direct approach with him. "I'll take another five thousand."

The casino manager cleared his throat and squeezed his pug nose, as if holding back a sneeze.

"That will be all," Leslie pleaded. "I just want to win my money back. It will take that much to do it."

"Are you sure?"

"Yes."

"Okay," he said. "You can make good, right?"

"I've never owed a penny in my life to anyone."

"We're not talking pennies," he grunted.

"Of course," Leslie said. "Besides, I wouldn't waste your time or mine with such small stakes." Sometimes she affected a tough posture to soften a hard person. The response was generally bafflement or, if the person saw through the act, a protective feeling.

"Okay," he joked. "Pennies are for piggy banks. They don't even fit into the slot machines."

Moving to another table, Leslie prayed for a reverse of the run of bad luck. The casino was emptying out. Even the slot machines were silent, with no more quarters cascading out of them. Now she was matched one-on-one with the dealer. The five stacks of a thousand each sat in a row before her. She played three hands, a pile on each, losing two and tying on the third, which she left there and won on the next bet. A group of people fidgeted behind her. Out of the corners of her eyes Leslie searched for any hotel guests who might whisper at breakfast about the gambling spectacle they were witnessing on the island. The only recognizable face was that of the housewife from the other blackjack table. *Get away from here. It's cruel how you take pleasure from my pain*, Leslie screamed in her head. No sound came out. The chips, weightless in her hand, vanished in an instant. Cashing in the last hundred-dollar chip for four twenty-fives, Leslie held on tightly before releasing them, blowing on each one like a tennis player drying her sweaty fingers before a serve. The casino man reappeared, holding up his hands to indicate that he was closing up shop, out of chips. Leslie cashed in the five-dollar chip the dealer had thrown her, like a dog's bone, for one last try.

"Come with me," the casino manager commanded in a soft, almost bereaved voice.

Staggering out of her chair, she followed him into a chilly office with air conditioning that lifted yellow sack curtains. He motioned Leslie to sit down and then placed a pen and white forms with carbon sheets on her side of the desk.

"You owe us ten thousand dollars," he said coolly, shredding her original check for two grand. "I take it the check is no good."

She nodded sheepishly. Leslie had never bounced a check in her whole life. It had been her intention earlier in the evening to make a swift profit and then rip up the check after giving the casino cash for it.

"I don't have that kind of money," she said. "I couldn't have lost that much. I only arrived a short while ago."

"You've been playing for three and a half hours."

Oddly, Leslie felt lightheaded, almost relieved, as though she had been massaged instead of spanked.

"What do I do?"

"Fill out these forms," he ordered, holding the pages down with the force of his forefingers. She scribbled her name, address, place of work and signature. The handwriting seemed distant, as if it did not belong to her.

"Listen," Leslie begged. "I don't want my parents to know about this. They'd kill me."

Cocking his sullen eyebrow, he looked sideways at her and replied, "No problem. Just get me the money. It's between you and me. No one else knows anything. There are no leaks. I run this whole operation. Just get me the money."

"I don't have it."

"Find it . . . *before* you leave."

He handed her a card reading EDDIE HARMON, CASINO MANAGER, ANLUCIA. Leslie had not thought to ask for it, considering him someone with no connection to her life. In return he demanded to hold on to her press card as collateral. It had taken her years to earn the credential, and now she was throwing it away in the casino, putting it in his grubby hands. All that she had built for herself seemed to collapse as easily as a lopsided pile of chips. In a sense Leslie had lost her future long ago. "You have no critical judgment," her father attacked her, after disagreeing with a movie review she had written the first day of her first newspaper job. "You haven't seen enough movies in your life to know what you're talking about." Since that time all the raises and promotions had felt like firings. Any promise in her life would be merely a stroke of luck.

With his glacial blue eyes on her, Eddie Harmon instructed, "Be here tomorrow at six sharp. I want a progress report."

Escorting Leslie to the door, he put her in a cab and handed the driver a bill. "Take her to Sandy Cove," he said. For ten thousand dollars Leslie was given a free ride back to the hotel.

"How long you be here on deh island," the driver asked.

"After tonight," she sighed, "I don't know how long."

"You lose your money up to deh casino," he said merrily. "Tomorrow you try your luck again, mahn."

Leslie turned silent, staring at rows of Long John trees, their calyxes gyrating to earth like small helicopters. She rolled up the car window, denying herself a caress from the tender tropical night.

She handed the driver her last five dollars as a tip and closed the door quietly. Afraid that her footsteps might awaken her parents, Leslie removed her sandals and tiptoed barefoot past their cottage to her room. Rebecca, her back to the door, was sound asleep. Dazed, Leslie lay on the bed fully dressed, her mind jumping like the chameleon on the beamed ceiling overhead.

8

As the darkness was edged out of the sky, the gunmetal dawn turned to silvery gray. Leslie tried to sleep but kept falling into fitful naps that left her even more exhausted. She recalled something about the casino, but could not be sure, thinking maybe she had dreamed it. She was feeling the effects of too much wine and too many cigarettes. Her brain was fuzzy. Turning her head restlessly on the pillow, she caught a glimpse of the sea, its dark outline churning up angry white foam. The waves dragged her back to the desperation she had felt as she walked from the cab to her door. How easy it would be to throw herself into the sea. The undertow was powerful and could accomplish its death mission in a matter of minutes. She was already pulled down by events, images of herself desperately combing the bottom of her pocketbook for chips and spilling them on the table. Her mind rehearsed various scenarios, whether to tell the family about the gambling disaster or hide it from them.

Should she just blurt it out or deliver an elaborate monologue on the pain that had led to this situation. Her body shuddered at the thought of a confession, and she curled up in a fetal position under a bundle of blanket, pulling it over her head to shut out the nascent day.

It seemed as if just a few minutes had passed when she felt a poke. Rebecca, with specks of sand-encrusted lotion all over her sunburned body, stood over the bed. "Get up," she nudged. "It's noon."

Disoriented, Leslie straddled some elusive time zone that gave her vertigo and brought her close to tears. The blinding force of the sun startled her. She rubbed her eyes and then shut them to yellow dots floating above her nose.

"Where did you go last night?" Rebecca scolded. "When I got back to the room you weren't here."

Leslie ransacked her brain for a believable excuse. "I fell asleep on the beach," she stammered. "By the time I opened my eyes it was almost dawn."

Rebecca sat down on the bed and studied her hands. She coiled a loose thread around her finger and picked at a perception. "You have to forget about Adam," she began tentatively. "Just put him out of your mind completely."

Leslie was relieved that her sister had come up with a theory that deflected her from what was really the matter and gave Leslie time to pull herself together for the moment.

"You should get up now," Rebecca persisted. "There's probably no toothpaste left. I told you to bring your own. You used up all of mine. You shouldn't squeeze it from the middle either."

Any gratitude Leslie felt for her sister's concern was short-lived. She was in no mood for a lecture on travel etiquette. How easy it was, too, for Rebecca to give out these instructions. Her life was about discarding men or keeping them at a cool distance. Any show of emotion, according to Rebecca, was an act of desperation. "Are you finished with your spiel?" Leslie blurted.

Rebecca backed off. The stern look on her face eased into a forced cheerfulness. "Come outside," she said. "It's beautiful. Hurry. I'll tell Mommy you'll be out right away."

Leslie kicked back the bedcovers. If she could just dress herself, then maybe she would be in a better position to deal with her problem. Or at the very least she would be less inclined to fall back to sleep. Bending down to get her bathing suit out of the dresser, she felt dizzy. She dropped the suit on the bed and sat next to it. Slowly, she lifted one leg, then the other, to pull it on.

As she came out of the cottage, she watched the family, chatting among themselves, on the beach. She waved broadly, hoping to ward off any suspicions about her behavior. By now Rebecca, an unregenerate tattletale, had probably given a full report on the previous night. Oddly, her father would have no comment on Leslie rising at noon. Whenever the family stayed out late he always insisted that his wife and daughters rest the next day while he settled for a catnap. With a quick glance over the shoulder he would stride out of the house to conquer the world while the women slept.

Her mother greeted Leslie. "You missed breakfast. You better get something to eat." She had a way of turning the holiday into a summer camp schedule.

Leslie snatched at the suggestion and walked off in the direction of the dining room. A waitress, trudging through the sand in white nurse's shoes, motioned to her. Leslie quickened her pace to remove herself from hearing range of the family.

"Dere's a phone call for you," the waitress said.

Leslie prayed it was Adam. She always developed a telepathy about lovers and instinctively knew when to get in touch with them. Thus far no one had been similarly wired to her needs. She held onto a hope, her only connection, tenuous as it was, that Adam might be on the line.

Her heart was going like a jackhammer. Reaching across the front desk to grab the phone, she thought she heard long-distance static on the line, but realized the sound was coming from inside her head.

"Hello," said a voice she did not recognize as Adam's.

"Who is this?" Leslie asked dejectedly.

"Eddie . . . Be at the casino at six sharp." He clicked off instantly.

She held the phone at arm's length as though to distance herself from the message. The clerk looked disapprovingly at her. "Are you tru, ma'am?" she asked. "We be hav to keep deh line open for uddah guests."

Leslie nodded vacantly at the woman. Her knees began to wobble, and she struggled to stay on her feet. Off the lobby she heard silverware being put on tables and remembered she was on her way to eat. That gave her some place to go. She felt clumsy and unattractive as she made her way into the dining room and collapsed in the nearest chair. Momentary images of herself in the casino filled the gray space between her skull and brain, but were quickly dismantled by rushes of conflicting plots to save herself. She sat rocking her head in upturned palms. The straw placemat cut into her elbows. Opening her eyes, she saw two efficient black hands, belonging to a waitress, setting water and napkins on the table. A menu was crooked under her arm, and she clicked a ballpoint to take Leslie's order.

"What's the fastest thing to make?" Leslie inquired, wanting to finish the meal before the family could join her.

"Dah tuna salad."

"Fine," she replied distractedly, "I'll have that, please."

She ground her teeth on the bed of lettuce. Each chunk of tuna felt tough and dry. She forced it down her throat with baby sips of iced tea. The waitress slid the check under the butter plate. Leslie jabbed it with her signature and got up from the table.

Back on the beach the sand was scorching. The heat was building to an intolerable level, so stifling as not to allow an opening for a trade wind to sail through. The sun streaming behind clouds cast a yellowish humidity over the sea, which turned a milky lime color. She could taste the excesses of the previous night. Smells of alcohol and cigarettes oozed out of her sweaty pores and laced her saliva. A tingling pain snaked down the side of her face. It flashed inside her eyes like heat lightning. Her tremors were hot shivers. Leslie plunged into the water to pump her system clean. The sea kept churning up sand that made it difficult to breathe or to see underwater. She swam farther out, paddling clumps of seaweed behind her. Her head was now throbbing, shudders of pain and then a massive thud. Leslie was sure she was having a cerebral hemorrhage.

At this moment she would not mind dying. Suicide had always been pegged to a specific event, the loss of a job or lover. Then it became a passing thought, and in more recent times an alternative to life itself. It occurred to Leslie that living was a vicious cycle, now that she wanted to kill herself over money squandered in the casino. She waited for a colossal wave to claim her body, but instead gentle ripples propelled her slowly toward shore.

She plopped down on the chaise longue and ordered a cool peanut crunch to wake herself up. The drink was so cold that her forehead tingled as she swallowed it.

Rebecca was arguing with her father about a couple twirling around in the water in an embrace.

"A lot of older women like younger men," Rebecca explained.

"It's moronic," he said. "What would a young boy want with an older woman?"

It amazed Leslie that her father would engage in such a

pedestrian argument. But he always needed to get in the last word, wherever.

"If older men can have younger women," Rebecca protested, "women should be able to do the same. You're just jealous."

He grinned, his expression one of both indignation and ridicule. "Me," he laughed. "You must have some crazy imagination."

"Oh, please!" Rebecca huffed. Clearly, the older-woman-younger-man theme was another notch on her feminist belt.

The conversation amused and had a calming effect on Leslie. Drifting off in thought, she suddenly saw an answer to her casino problem. For some reason she remembered a lesbian loan shark she knew back in New York. Maybe she should write and ask her for an interview, chronicling her courageous foray into hitherto all-male territory while subtly hitting her up for a ten-thousand-dollar loan.

Leslie scratched her head and considered that no matter how quickly she could dash off the letter there was no way to speed up the mail on the island. Assuming that the note reached Ms. Foster, she would still need a couple of days of sweet-talking her into a loan. For all she knew, too, the loan shark had blown her last ten thousand on a chorus person. Meanwhile, Casino Eddie of Anlucia was kicking for the money—right now! She could not call to mind Foster's unlisted number and figured it had probably been changed for the tenth time.

Moving rapidly away from that scheme and more in the direction of Cottage 18, Leslie saw that the door was wide open. It was one of the few rooms with an entrance at the side rather than facing the beach. Usually its occupants, a kindly old couple, sat spendthrift of time under a thatched umbrella. One afternoon Leslie had tea with them in their room and was astonished to see an enormous pear-shaped diamond ring sitting in an ashtray with a safety pin. She liked the woman's soft curls, with a tint of blue to them, and the courtly way, verging on vaudeville, the husband treated her, going inside to fetch her a sweater as the sun died for the day. Now they were nowhere in sight. The man, who sat with his knees apart and ankles touching, always had a smile for passers-by. At first Leslie thought it was just friendliness. But when she saw him walk out of the room in underpants instead of bathing trunks one morning, she recognized the perpetual grin as the onset of senility.

Seeking an escape from the family, she thought she would drop by to say hello to the couple. She got up and walked across the patch of lawn, past the shuffleboard area, to their cottage. Circling it twice, as though poking around to see if anyone was home, she was concerned that the door should be wide open like that. Not wanting to trespass, of course, but also realizing her duties as a watchful neighbor, Leslie entered the room to check it out. No sign of anyone, but there was the sound of running water in the sink inside the bathroom. She peeked through a crack in the door too narrow to provide a clue. On her hands and knees she attempted to look under the door, spotting the ropelike ends of a mop. Slowly, quietly, Leslie got up from the floor and tiptoed over to the bureau. A clean job, she figured, just a little rifling through the nighties and garter belts for some cold cash. Suddenly the bathroom door swung open. A robust housekeeper, picking up her mop, stared at Leslie and asked nonchalantly, "You checking in, mahn?"

"Uh, uh, no . . . I was concerned about the people in here."

"Who are dey?"

"My friends," Leslie stammered, "the old couple."

"Oh, dat party, dey be check out dis morning," she reported. "Dah lady, she faint. She hav weak heart and he take her bahk home."

Oblivious to her surroundings reeling before her, Leslie zigzagged out of the cottage. "Oh, my God," she muttered, clenching her fists to claim an emotion, whether it be relief at not completing her desperate plan or panic at what to do next.

She looked up and saw her mother, who shook Leslie's shoulders and said, "You're completely white. What's the matter?"

"You know that nice old couple," Leslie babbled. "The woman had a heart attack and had to go home."

"What a pity," her mother said, half-listening. "Your father thought we'd better eat before it gets any later."

"What time is it anyway?"

"Close to three. Are you coming in for lunch?"

Leslie shuddered at the thought of food and family. "I just ate." She shrugged.

Leslie returned to the cottage and fell down on the bed. Dizzy and nauseated, she rushed into the bathroom and threw up. To hide any further evidence of upset from Rebecca, she sprayed the toilet bowl with cologne. She opened the medicine chest and saw that her makeup consisted of a lipstick. She removed Rebecca's toiletry case and looked inside it for mascara and eyeshadow. Her sister rarely used makeup, but always packed everything as if stockpiling for a nuclear attack. Leslie scratched the bottom of the sink with the mascara brush to check the color—a light brown. A shade darker would go better with Leslie's complexion, but she figured she could get away with this in the dimly lit casino. The eyeshadow, melting from the heat, felt like a crushed crayon, too messy, which was why Leslie almost never bothered with it. She peeled off her bathing suit and got into the shower. The hot water, turned on full force, pounded the tension out of her back. Draped in a towel, Leslie opened the closet and reviewed her wardrobe for the evening. She chose a white caftan, soft and feminine, yet loose-fitting enough to give her mobility. If she had no power over her life at this moment, at least she was free to decide what to wear to the casino. Leslie did not bother to rehearse the conversation, so convinced was she that her troubles would be over just as soon as she could get to a phone. She cursed the fact that there were none for outside calls in the rooms. In another hour, though, she consoled herself, the lobby would be empty of guests. Everyone would be either drinking or taking a siesta, and she could call from the conference room behind the front desk. She set her alarm for four o'clock and took a nap.

When she awoke she felt refreshed and hopeful as she stuffed her telephone credit card inside her bathing suit. As she passed her parents' cottage she saw that their blinds were closed. Rebecca, socializing on the main terrace, would probably not spot her.

Leslie hurried to the front desk. "I want to make a long-distance call," she said. "Will you accept a credit card here? I don't want it to show up on the bill."

"Yes," the clerk said.

"Look," Leslie instructed, "please don't mention my calling anyone if you see my family around."

"No problem," the clerk replied. "What tis dah number?"

Leslie would talk to anyone willing to wire her ten thousand dollars immediately to cover her debt. No number came up. How many people, after all, would consider a gambler a good credit risk? Friendships could be wiped out in an instant over a loan. Picking the right digits would be sheer luck.

The operator came on the line almost immediately. The clerk motioned Leslie to pick up the call in the conference room. A black phone with a long cord sat in the middle of the huge rectangular table. Before pulling it toward her, she yanked the miniature curtains closed over a narrow row of windows bordering the ceiling. The room fronted the driveway, which was deserted and quiet. But Leslie did not want to take any chances and switched on the air conditioner to mute her voice. Wet with perspiration, she moved away from where the air was blowing to avoid catching cold. Then she lunged for the phone, shoving the receiver against her ear.

The dial tone sounded like a snore with crickets caught in the line. It range once, twice, three times, like labored breathing. Then a strange person picked up on the other end of the line.

"Hello, hello," Leslie yelled into the phone. She heard her own echo. "Is Joe there?"

"No," the man said, "the restaurant is closed now. We shut down for a few days over the holiday."

"When could I reach him?"

"Who is calling, please?"

"A friend."

Apparently that was a sufficient answer. "Mr. Manno is in Las Vegas. He won't be returning until after the New Year."

"Oh," Leslie said. The air conditioner had a slight convulsion and began to shake and make loud noises.

"Can I give him a message?"

Leslie dropped the phone down on its cradle. Stunned, she raced out of the room and asked the clerk to get the operator back. Now she picked up the phone again to call out another number. But the man from the restaurant was still on the line. She jammed the button with her whole fist to disconnect.

"Are you tru wit the call, ma'am," the operator asked calmly.

"Yes, please, please," she begged. "I want to make another call."

"I hav to get bahk to you in a minute."

There was no better cash business than owning a restaurant or club. But if Joe, who ran her favorite place in the town, was "cash rich," one trip to Vegas could make him cash-poor overnight. It made no sense to track him down there. She would have to page him at the crap table. She knew how much Joe loved the action; he would not give up his spot to take the call.

She grabbed the phone and tugged at the three numbers required to get the operator. He got on the line and said there were two calls before hers. She felt like she was down to three chips and forced to wait while the casino manager went to get the forms for the markers. It was interminable. Jumping out of her seat, she walked out to the front desk and asked the clerk to try to get the operator back for her.

"He's not answering just now."

"Jesus," Leslie moaned, holding her head in her hands and rolling it around.

Back in the conference room she dialed the operator herself. She kept getting a busy. Then Leslie started to direct-dial. The operator came on the line.

"What tis dah probelem?"

"I'm trying to get through," she hollered. "I've been waiting twenty minutes."

"Tis not easy to get tru," he said, his voice registering an annoyance that could mean deliberate stalling.

Talking tough was not the right approach. Unkinking her tight voice, Leslie said apologetically, "I know how difficult it must be. I really appreciate how you are trying for me."

"Okay, ma'am, I do my best."

"Five one six, three seven four, five two seven nine."

Leslie's tennis partner was a big builder, successful enough to conduct his business while lying in bed. He lived in a Marcel Breuer home on a three-acre plot on the harbor. In the driveway there were "his" and "hers" Mercedes Benzes. On the court he was always talking up big deals.

Now she would find out if he put his money where his mouth was.

"Hello."

"This is Leslie. Is Jerry there?"

"Oh, hi," his wife said. "You sound far away. Where are you?"

His wife, who played tennis three times a week and shopped the other two weekdays, did not know how to budget time. The call might well stretch into the yenta hour. Her knowledge bank consisted of knowing designer labels and names of specialists. She was always on a diet which necessitated a lot of trips to the doctor to check her blood pressure.

"I'm in the islands," Leslie said.

"Which one?"

"Anlucia."

"Is it important?" she inquired. "He had a meeting in the city today."

"Will he be back by six?" Leslie implored. Time was running out. She wanted to be able to go to Casino Eddie with a firm commitment to pay up.

"I never know with him," she said. "His schedule is so unpredictable. My guess is the meeting will run into dinner. But I could have him call you as soon as he gets in. What's your number?"

"Oh, no," Leslie said, trying to sound unperturbed, "that's not necessary. I just wanted to tell him I ran into someone who has a property that might interest him."

It was too risky to leave a message for Jerry to call back. He knew the family and might ask for someone else in Leslie's absence.

"Are you having fun?" his wife said. "Jerry and I are going away in February."

"The weather is lovely."

"I'm so jealous," she whined. "It's cold and rainy here. I

told Jerry to move his business to Florida or some place that's warm.''

"Okay,'' Leslie sighed. ''I'll see you when I get back.''

Click. The cheerfulness in her voice collapsed into sobs. Like a bereaved person trying to keep up a calm front, Leslie grieved alone. It seemed that there was no one left in the world to help her. Even with her salary, she would not be eligible for a ten-thousand-dollar loan. Her parents had always financed cars and home improvements, so she had had no opportunity to establish credit through a previous loan. She had only gotten markers at the casino on account of the family's good name, a privilege that now infuriated her.

She decided to call Rachel, her agent, who was forever trying to wean Leslie from a safe magazine job and into more independent projects. The woman was brilliant and given to screaming at stupidity, and in no time Leslie had made her into a surrogate father. She was counting now on Rachel to extract a hefty advance, at least ten thousand, from John Frank, a television network vice-president high on a script Leslie did on working heiresses. Eagerly, Leslie dialed her agent.

"Hi, Rachel,'' she said. ''What's going on with my script?''

"No word as yet.''

"What do you mean? It's been on that guy's desk a whole month.''

"That's not so long.''

"It is for *me*,'' Leslie shot back. ''I need ten thousand immediately. I'm in the most serious imaginable situation.''

Rachel hedged. ''Can you tell me what it's about?''

"Not right now.'' Leslie hesitated. ''One day I'll tell you the whole story. But, believe me, it's serious, and I mean *dead* serious.''

"Well . . .'' Rachel sort of hummed, nervously. ''This is

an impossible time. Nothing gets done over the holidays.''

"That guy is always on holiday,'' she muttered angrily, "if he's not out to lunch.''

Rachel paused and then advised coolly, "Time is of the essence.''

Exasperated, Leslie said, "I'll call him myself then.''

"You won't be able to reach him.''

"What?'' Leslie exploded. "I can track down anyone. I'll get him on the phone in two seconds. I haven't been a reporter for ten years for nothing.''

"If I were you,'' Rachel warned, "I wouldn't do that. In fact, I'm telling you not to.''

"Just give me one good reason why not,'' Leslie shouted.

Rachel's apparent calm was confusing, if not altogether disconcerting. By now, Leslie figured, she should have blown a fuse. Something was wrong.

Rachel blurted it out. "John Frank was fired last Monday.''

"What?'' Leslie was stunned. She could feel the blood drain out of her face.

Rachel never skipped a chance to turn a disappointment into an object lesson and launched into her all-time favorite spiel. "What did I tell you, kiddo: Never love a corporation because it doesn't love you back.''

Leslie pressed her. "Who's his replacement? Did you call him? What did he say?''

"I thought it best to wait until he gets settled into the job.'' Rachel sighed. "At this point he probably can't find anything on his desk.''

"What's his name?'' Leslie seethed. "You mean you haven't even tried to reach him?''

Reluctantly, her agent confessed. "Leslie, I called twice, and both times he was tied up in meetings.''

"Yeah,'' muttered Leslie weakly, backing off from any further bad news.

"We'll get a sale," Rachel comforted. "The script is really very good."

"Okay," Leslie murmured, too stunned to persevere.

"Try to enjoy the rest of your stay," Rachel said, adding, "I didn't call because I thought it might ruin your holiday."

"Bye," Leslie said, her voice wavering. She wrapped her arms around the phone and began to weep. Between sobs, she wondered why she could not bring herself to tell Rachel about the gambling. And what of her other attempts to get the money? They seemed so feeble now. Was it shame that prevented her from going to her parents, who could easily come up with the cash? Or might it be arrogance? Leslie had a self-image of someone with money, the smarts to get more or, at the very least, to hold on to it. She could not afford a confession. So often she had felt like a supplicant before her father, who always imputed foolish and reckless needs to her requests and invariably rejected her explanations. His suspicious interrogations goaded Leslie to achieve on her own, so she would no longer be subjected to his unpredictable largesse. The free round-trip ticket to the island was more a command appearance than a gift, especially since Leslie might have preferred to remain behind. Now she had a good reason to want a handout. Good and stupid, she berated herself, just as her father surmised. She shed tears of self-pity as she recalled her struggle to be professionally successful and emotionally independent. It was as if she had just swept away ten years of building self-esteem in the face of her father's on-and-off contempt. She had wanted to become her own person, but was forever pulled back by her need for his approval. That very need had created a mess for her now.

She began dialing a few combinations of digits, belonging to various friends and colleagues, without lifting the receiver. Before one number returned to its proper slot, she had already started another.

"Operator," Leslie said solemnly, "please call four one five, six five two, four five seven two."

"What is dat?"

"California . . . the San Francisco area."

Adam answered on the first ring. What was the purpose of the call? Adam did not have that kind of cash handy, and she would never ask him for it under any circumstances. She wished, though, that she could rest her head on his shoulder, and that he would hold it up.

"What?" Adam said.

"This is Leslie." Her heart beat like a metronome.

"How are you?"

"Okay," she said, holding back tears. "I mean, not so great."

"What's the matter?" he asked softly, his concern giving Leslie momentary comfort.

"I don't know."

"Where are you?"

"Anlucia."

"With the family," he snapped.

"Yes," she said weakly.

This long-standing date with the family had become a habit, one that Adam discouraged by refusing to go along. He treated these visits like an infidelity, and despite repeated promises to change her ways, she could not achieve the closure with her parents that other people her age had. As a result she suffered from guilt and confusion. Sometimes on her way home the only seat left on the train faced the direction opposite to where she was going, mirroring the pull in her own mind. By the time Leslie could decide to turn around, they had already passed the station where she might have made the connection. But for now, she knew the family would claim this child—momentarily lost to someone else—at her stop.

He breathed impatience into the phone. "It serves you right," he scolded.

"Adam," she pleaded, "why are you being so cruel?"

"Why do you do it to yourself?" he protested. "I can't help you."

"What does that mean?"

"Exactly what it means," he said coldly. "I'm on my way out the door for cocktails. I've been cooped up in my studio all day."

"Adam," she began.

He cut her off. "I can't believe you went on that family holiday," he smoldered. "You deserve whatever you get."

"Bye." Leslie could not find any other words. Her voice went dead. Adam was already off the line when the phone rolled out of her hand onto the table.

She staggered from his words back to the room. She dressed hurriedly, before depression could knock her out for the night. She stepped outside into a growing darkness that dropped a cool curtain over the island. She got in the car, idling it out of the driveway. Through her confusion she saw one thing clearly. Adam was right. She never should have come. Hunched over the steering wheel, she studied the road unfolding ahead, rolling on under the night, and her mind shifted back to a time when she might have saved herself from all this grief.

9

---

*"All week long it had been gray and damp with light
spring rain, uncommon for this time of year. Hansom
cabs, with wreaths and couples in blankets, moved
regally up and down my avenue. Street people looking
up at my life through the living-room picture windows
might have imagined a glossy, sophisticated existence, something quite apart from the person residing
here. I had the floors polished and put in a few plants,
for you. My phone was out of order, and not heard to
ring in two hours. Though I could dial out, there was
nothing incoming. Still no word from you. I called the
phone company to scream. Then I rewatered the
plants, made myself another cup of hot chocolate,
rinsed the same glass a third time in the sink, arranged
my slippers in place by the bed, inserted a Cole Porter
record back into its jacket, rubbed cream into my
eyelids, changed the towels on the bathroom rack and*

threw out a half-empty container of orange juice. A repairman in a black hooded jacket appeared an hour later. I worried that his hands, with grease frozen into red knuckles, would dirty my white phone, all dusted and perfumed to send my scent to you. It was almost ten at night. I gave him a glass of soda and a cracker with a cream cheese and caviar dip, your favorite. He sat for a few minutes and became my company, waiting to hear from central office. They restored my service, but they could not repair my life, with all its disconnections, particularly from you. The phone rang. It was my brother Jason's wife asking about a job contact. I was brief, wanting to keep the line open for you. An hour or two passed, and then I went next door, to Rumpelmayer's, a mix of stuffed animals, baby-pink wallpaper and aging spinsters. I sat at the counter with old ladies, listened as they ordered tea, crumpets and conversations from the soda men. Fred, tall, white-haired and with stiltlike movements, asked if you were coming for Christmas. Without a word I paid the check for a vanilla malted—I lost my resolve to diet—and returned to the apartment. I ran the bath water again and stepped into the tub, and even that did not make the phone ring. I started to write a letter to you, then fell asleep. I rose in the middle of the night and packed my suitcase by the phone. In the morning I turned only one lock on the door just in case my phone rang on the way to the elevator and I had to get back in quickly. Then I caught the plane to the island where, this evening, I have my answer. Goodbye, Adam."

10

Leslie blotted a tear in the rearview mirror to keep her mascara from running. The red traffic light, hanging precariously from a lopsided wire, changed, and she swung a right, gunning the car to climb the steep hill to the casino. She switched on the high beams to spill light onto the pitch-black driveway. The car spun around on the gravel as she hit the brake to ease it into a parking slot. Leslie sat for a moment and stared at the fingernail moon. She reached inside her dress and dried her underarms with a tissue. Then she got out of the car and walked the few steps, pebbles crunching underfoot, to the casino entrance. Its brass door, sealed shut, felt cold and unyielding as she struggled to pull it open, grabbing the huge ring handle that would not give. Moving her hand up and down the rough stone facade, she felt around for a doorbell. She heard the silence and was reminded of the funereal mood that transposed nervous laughter into prehysterical giddiness.

She rapped on the door and listened for footsteps on the other side. A spotlight fell on the driveway and then she heard a key turning the latch. Eddie flung open the door, holding it with an outstretched arm as Leslie edged her body into the casino, careful not to bump against him.

"Hi," he said absently. "I'm on a long-distance call. Make yourself comfortable. I'll only be a few minutes."

He darted back into his brightly lit office, leaving Leslie to pace the cavernous room. The carpet cushioned her determined steps. The tables were bare, empty of chips, canisters and cards. Without the chandeliers spreading rainbow light refractions over the room the place looked dreary. She felt like a mole inside the windowless space, lit only by sickly fluorescent bulbs near the cashier's cage. The smell of polish on the brass rails mingled with a floral room freshener. The casino seemed to lie in wait for the next batch of gamblers.

Leslie stepped into a shard of light coming from Eddie's half-open door. He spotted her and beckoned her into his office, stretching the phone cord to walk around the desk and pull out a chair for her. "I'll be another sec," he whispered, holding his hand over the phone. He squatted in front of a liquor cabinet and poured himself a drink, then held up the glass as an invitation for Leslie to join him. She moved her hand laterally to reject the offer. Eddie winked. Her hand dropped in her lap. Unwittingly, Leslie had just given the gambler's signal to refuse another card and stick on the bet.

"What do you figure—end of January? February?" Eddie said, now adjusting the phone to his other ear. "I may be working on a deal from this end that'll get me out of here faster."

Leslie's neck felt stiff as she swept the room with a few quick glances to get a fix on Eddie. The decorations were limited to a few doodles on a desk blotter and a photo of a boy, probably about fifteen, wearing a football helmet and uniform. It was hard to believe she was in the same room as last night. There was little of the sinister manner that had so terrified her.

Eddie shook a cigarette out of a fresh pack and reached across the desk to offer it to her. She fumbled for the cigarette. As he stetched his body to remove a gold lighter from his pants pocket, Leslie observed that he was remarkably fit, his stomach completely flat. She took a long puff on the cigarette and thought she would lose her breath. A smell as if from a burning paper cup filled her nostrils. She had inserted the wrong end of the cigarette in her mouth. Crushing it out, she swatted the air in front of her face.

"By the way, Vince is getting antsy," Eddie said, shuffling another cigarette out of the pack, this time handing it to her. "But I assured him it wouldn't be too much longer, one way or another, and told him to hop a seaplane over here in the meantime. It'll be a change, even if all these damn islands look alike. Okay, I'll be back to you on it. Talk to you soon."

Eddie grimaced at the phone as he hung up and then checked his digital watch. "The damn phone never stops. I'm hungry. Where should we go for dinner?"

What in hell, Leslie wondered, was going on? It was as if Casino Eddie had already forgotten why she was here. Or was this some kind of perverse game? Though her terror was receding fast, she was reluctant to trust her luck. She thought maybe she should bring up the money now as protection against his suddenly springing it on her later and catching her off guard. The adrenaline rushing through Leslie would begin to fall off, eventually quitting for the night. She took a deep breath as if to recharge her courage.

Eddie's voice penetrated her confusion. "Have you decided where yet?" he asked.

"I don't really know what to suggest in the way of restaurants," she demurred. "Usually I just eat at the hotel. You decide."

"Well, I have this place where I go if it's okay with you. It's called The Inn."

"Fine."

"The lady is so agreeable," he cracked.

Leslie had counted on returning to the hotel before anyone noticed her absence. She would have to call and leave word she had the car. She decided to phone from the restaurant without Eddie standing over her. Leslie paced in her mind, trying to decide whether to tell the family where she was or invent a lie. After wrestling with her guilt a few minutes, Leslie realized that, from her family's point of view, there was nothing particularly weird about her dining with a casino manager who looked like a cross between Jon Voight and Michael Moriarty, something Rebecca might do without a second's hesitation.

Eddie removed a navy blazer from a hanger on the back of the door and draped it over his arm. Before locking up, he pressed an intercom button, bent over to talk into the machine and announced, "I may be late. You open up. You've got the keys."

A voice responded: "See you later, boss."

As they stepped outside Eddie asked if they could use her car. "Mine's in the shop again."

"Sure." She got into the car and reached over to release the lock on the door on his side. He crawled in. Leslie turned the key and tapped the gas pedal.

"At the bottom of the hill we have to pull a right," Eddie instructed, "and then just follow that road about six miles, and we'll run into the restaurant."

The car lurched forward and almost hit the post holding the guard chains in the parking area. She gripped the steering wheel to try to steady herself.

Eddie reached over to check the gear shift. "You're in

drive," he said, jerking it into reverse. "Are you sure you don't want me to take over?"

"Maybe you should," Leslie mumbled, "because I don't even know where we're going and I'm not used to this dumb car."

The road was unlit and bordered by open fields. Somebody could be killed and dumped here, Leslie thought with a shudder, and no one would find her for years. She shivered and goose bumps broke out on her arms. "Could I use your jacket?" she asked.

"Sure, be my guest."

Slipping it over her shoulders, she grabbed hold of the lapels, tightly crumpling them with the tension in her fingers.

Eddie drove too fast with only one hand on the wheel. His other slapped the car roof and made a sound like a tin can popping. Leslie started, her heart pounding. She turned on the radio to distract herself.

The car wobbled over a pebbled driveway enclosed by brick walls with an overgrowth of ivy. It stopped at a fortresslike inn with a moat and gracefully appointed lawns sloping down to the landlocked harbor. Yachts from all over the world docked here. When the patrons made small talk, it was an exotic blend of French, English, German and the calypso dialect.

Eddie got out of the car and stretched, while Leslie removed his jacket and handed it back to him. "I wouldn't mind having a restaurant like this one day," he remarked as they walked through a bar to the outdoor dining patio.

They sat down at a table by the water. Light from candles in latticed holders dappled the cloth. Besides the sailors with their sun-bleached hair, there were several young families and a few single people her own age. Leslie had an affinity for yachtsmen who gambled with the high seas and winds. Guests at the hotel where the family stayed lacked the venturesome spirit of these boating types. "We like to come here," a businessman had told Leslie back at the hotel, "because we know where everything is . . . the tennis court, the beach, the dining room. I gamble every day in my business. We're here to relax, not to take silly risks."

Leslie was pleased that Eddie chose such a charming and subdued place. She almost had to remind herself to be nervous. There was something unsyncopated about Eddie. The boyishly handsome face was disfigured by smoky bags under his eyes—the result of either trouble or age. He had good straight teeth, but the tight droop of his lower lip toughened his smile. If not for the slouch of his walk, he almost could have seemed preppy, in khaki trousers, a blue Lacoste shirt and blazer slung over the shoulder.

They ordered rum swizzles, a barbecued steak dinner for Eddie and fresh swordfish for Leslie. A twenty-member steel band was warming up as if they were members of a symphony orchestra. Ranging in age from preteens to grandparents, the musicians wore bright-colored print shirts with a gold diamond design. One of the kids sported a red Adidas running jacket some New York jogger had probably left on the beach. The little ones wore incongruous wool stocking caps.

Leslie liked the melodious throbbing of the steel band in the tropical night. Yacht masts swaying in the harbor created a timpanic background. People stood, like birds preening, waiting for the music to start. They were casual, barefooted, no one with anyone in particular, old and young, unselfconscious, keeping a perfect beat. It was like watching a primitive rite. The biceps of the maraca player bulged from the tension of shaking an instrument that looked like a loaf of bread and produced a sandpaper sound.

"Do you sail?" Leslie wondered aloud.

"I do a little skimming over the shallow water in an outboard," he said shyly. "Otherwise, as close as I get to the sea is on a beach mat. I'm a Midwesterner."

Eddie asked her to dance. His hands were smooth and his motions graceful. The way he held her, with both arms around her waist gently pressing her close, felt good after Adam's rebuke. It was dawning on her there might well be an easy and pleasurable solution to this horrible mess. She was glad that she had on a dress instead of pants and wondered if her perfume was still detectable.

His arm was still clutching her waist when they returned to the table. She excused herself to call and leave a message for the family and then go to the bathroom, where she put on a fresh coat of lipstick, fluffed her hair and misted herself with a pocket-size perfume atomizer to revive the aroma. She lifted her breasts inside the caftan to reveal more cleavage and rehearsed some dance steps before the mirror that stretched the length of the sink wall. She gave herself a final inspection and, seeing her forehead creased with worry, suddenly remembered this was not high-school prom night. At least, she kidded herself, she had a date now.

Eddie beamed as she walked toward him. He sniffed her perfume appreciatively as he leaned over to pull out her chair. An elderly black man, with huge pink gaps of gum where teeth had once been and tufts of gray hair shooting out of his head like electrical wires, stood deferentially, his hands crisscrossed over his chest, a few steps from her chair. As he spoke he leaned backward, away from her. "Aren't you one of dah Rittmahn fahmily?"

"Yes," Leslie blinked.

"You doesn't remember me," he quizzed her. "I'm Winston."

"Oh, sure," she replied politely, repeating his name to give credibility to her lie. "Winston. Sure."

"I tought I recognized you," he said gleefully. "I used to drive dah fahmily when you all was real small. How is dah judge and your mothah?"

"Great."

"Tell dem all hello," Winston said. "I be retired. I don't get down to dah Sandy Cove in a long time. But glad to hav you back with us." He bowed at the casino manager as an apology for the intrusion and then wandered back inside the bar.

Eddie, his head bent in thought, did not acknowledge the bow. He picked at a piece of lint curled like a spider on his trouser leg and arched his brow at her. "Your father and I have something in common."

"Ye-es," she replied, her voice traversing an octave, peaking to alarm, then sloping to anxious curiosity before reaching a middle ground of counterfeit affability.

"I almost became a lawyer," he said sulkily.

"Really?"

"Really," he said bitterly. "I did a semester of law school."

"How come you gave it up?"

"This criminal law professor," he began. "I worked part-time for him to pay my way through school. I was also waiting on tables."

"What happened?"

"I broke my ass for the guy," he snarled, "and he fucked me."

"How?"

"I was promised a fee for my work," he explained. "I helped with a case and was going round-the-clock on it—the week before exams, too. He had me trailing this broad in hotel lobbies, bugging the room and tapping her phone for the client. Forget about certain legalities—he didn't know from search warrants, *only* the fifty grand he got when the case was over. I asked him for my money, and the scumbag had the fucking nerve to tell me I was lucky I wasn't indicted. I wanted to kill him."

Leslie pressed his hand, imprinting it with the memory of

her own pain, the misery of manila envelopes, paperclips and pink slips.

He pulled away, apparently struggling to keep his emotions separate from hers. It reminded Leslie of someone withholding a laugh at a joke, sort of glaring at it. The cold response shut out the little hope she had of locating some compassion for her own situation inside his pain.

Glumly he recalled, "I already had two mouths to feed, a wife and kid. I started working with these people in Detroit who had other operations in Vegas and Miami. It wasn't exactly the law career I dreamed of. But the money was good. And the promotions came fast. I had no choice. Waiter, headwaiter, manager, helping with the books. Then they had this mess with the government, and I wound up in this tropical hole."

The conversation was making her uneasy. Please, God, she prayed, spare me the details. Yet she sensed that what was left out might be the problem, quicksand holes in the conversation into which she felt herself slipping, irretrievably. She thrashed about in her mind for a reply. "A lot of people go back to law school later," she fumbled. "Just because you had one bad steak, does it mean you have to swear off it forever?"

"Never mind filet mignon," Eddie shot back. "I'm talking about bad apples, every last one of these legal types."

His discontent was underscored by a humbled look, the kind that grew out of failed expectations and dimmed the eyes. There seemed to be no fight left in him. Maybe there never had been.

"Not all lawyers are corrupt," Leslie argued. "My father . . ."

Eddie cut her off. "Your father's a judge. It's not the same thing."

"What's not the same?" she asked incredulously. "You have to be a lawyer first."

"Nah." He waved her words away with the thrust of his hand.

Contempt swelled inside her head. She always lost patience with stupidity, particularly with know-it-alls, whose information was mostly erroneous, a defensive reaction like a tic.

But Eddie revealed instantly that he knew more than she might have suspected or, certainly, wanted him to. "Your old man's on the federal court. He's supposed to be above it all."

"He *is*," she boasted. Yet she could not help wondering what else Eddie knew. Was she being paranoid? She twitched, but then, realizing there was no dirty laundry, grabbed hold of herself. "No one could buy him. He never sat on boards of companies he represented or used inside information on stocks or exposed himself to conflicts of interest."

Sneering, he bumped her arm and cooed, "Hey—you're a big girl now. Why do you go on about your daddy so much?"

"Because I treasure him. I speak of other people who also matter to me." Despite her hurt, she would never betray her father to a stranger. Behind his back Leslie was always effusive in her praise and felt genuine in this. Perhaps she was too much of a coward to say these things to his face. She suspected that he, too, kept such proud feelings bottled up, until he could unleash them on a colleague by showing off Leslie's magazine articles. Compliments always arrived by way of third parties.

Eddie grabbed hold of her flailing hands, which had just missed toppling the wineglasses. "And he doesn't ride the backs of other people either," she continued excitedly. "He could leave everything for his law clerk, but he writes all his own decisions."

"At least someone's working," Eddie snorted. "But for

my money, the wheels of justice don't turn fast enough."
He deposited her hands back in her lap and playfully
spanked them.

"Why do you say that?"

"Just ask your father if he thinks people should be squatting in jail because some asshole prosecutor needs more
trial delays so he can chase after witnesses." He squinted
impatiently at her.

"Of course," Leslie declared, "he'd say it's wrong."

"Good," Eddie said dryly. "We're of the same mind,
then."

Like a dutiful schoolgirl she perked up, "The Sixth
Amendment, the right to a speedy trial. I should have gone
into law. Our dinner-table conversations were worth a law
school education."

"You'd have made a lot more money," he said, "That's
for sure."

"Not necessarily, because I would have worked for
the ACLU doing constitutional law, the only area that attracted me."

"Yeah," he snickered. "At school 'con law' is what we
all called it. That always amused me."

"How about torts?" Leslie joked. "It sounds like a
candy bar."

"Nah, con law is better." He sucked on a tooth. "It has a
special ring to it, sort of sums up the profession."

"Look," Leslie stated firmly, "all I know is that my
father is absolutely incorruptible. He puts in fifteen hours a
day and doesn't tolerate delays."

"Then maybe there's hope for all of us," he sighed. "My
father was the opposite. He was the only guy I knew who
took work breaks, between coffee."

"What did he do?"

"He had a luncheonette." Eddie shrugged. "He'd dump
all the dirty plates on Mom while he sat all day on that one

counter stool. He was too cheap to hire any extra help except whichever waitress he was banging. The girls were only a few years older than myself. He even dragged me in there from the time I was fourteen, after school and weekends. All my buddies were cuddling with their girls in booths and playing the jukebox and sharing sundaes while I was throwing eggs on English muffins. My wife was my first date."

"I'm sorry," Leslie blurted out.

"Don't be. My father left me a great legacy."

"What was that?"

"No one to live up to."

"Yes?" She did not know how else to respond. This was the saddest confession she had ever heard from anyone.

"You should have seen the way he bragged around to people who came into his luncheonette," Eddie seethed. " 'My boy, he's in law school.' They all figured he was footing the bills when the old guy wouldn't part with a dime for books. My mother was dead by then, either from broken arches or serving up ten thousand BLTs on white toast. He'd sooner have bought that waitress a few rounds of beer than help me."

"If it would mean anything to you," Leslie comforted, "you tried." She flicked her fingers, totaling the thousands of dollars her own father had spent on the childrens' schooling, travel and household luxuries. How did she, like Eddie, end up with a deck stacked against her? She felt like crying, but was too numbed.

The waiter reappeared with another round of drinks which Eddie seemed too quick to lift off the table. It crossed her mind, suddenly swerving from sympathy to concern about her own problem, to stick with a soda or water. Yet she felt more inclined at this moment to get tanked, to reach some distant state of oblivion. Slipping deeper into her seat, she stretched her legs, peeked down her dress and more or less gave herself the once-over.

Eddie twirled a straw in his drink and contemplated its whirlpool effect. "I'd be in great shape," he mused aloud, "if I had my own restaurant. Otherwise you get owned. I'm sure it's the same in fancy corporations like where you work. I may be able to pull it off if a few little things can be worked out. This way is no good. My life's not my own."

"Is your family here, too?"

"My son visits." Eddie beamed. "He's a helluva kid."

"You're divorced?"

"Yes." He shrugged. "My wife left me."

Eddie ran his fingers tensely through his silky blond hair. A strand fell across his forehead, something that Leslie always found sexy about men, otherwise all neat and symmetrical, no tits and ass hanging out of them. The piece dropped again, and Eddie flipped it back in place, fondling the hair as he matted it down. He took a long sip of his drink. "We had another son," he said sorrowfully. "He was born with brain damage. The kind that knocked the balance off. He had two operations on his—oh what's it called, damn it, I'll think of it."

"Cerebellum," Leslie said.

"That's it," Eddie replied, glancing admiringly at her. "Thanks."

Leslie hesitated. "Where is he now?"

Eddie chewed the cuticles around his thumb as if biting back tears. "He's dead two years. We knew he had a short life span but no one ever expected it to be over so soon. He fell on the concrete. My ex-wife wrote me about it in a letter. I didn't even get to go to my own son's funeral."

"She denied you this?" Leslie protested, cradling her face in upturned palms and rocking her head woefully.

Eddie stiffened as he spoke. "I don't blame her in a way," he said glumly. "I couldn't control my disappointment at Brian's not being able to play sports like other boys his age. I resented my son for something he couldn't help. My wife never forgave me. It was the start of the breakup of our marriage." He rubbed his pug nose, a perfect centerpiece on his Irish face, like a child trying to stop the sniffles after a cry. A tear stained his cheek, a salt-watery white bubble.

Leslie edged the cocktail napkin out from under her drink to offer up as a handkerchief, but it was soggy wet from the glass.

"My wife and I tried to get back together," Eddie continued, "but she found out about this girl I had on the side."

"Girl?" Leslie inquired facetiously. "I thought any female over eleven was a woman."

"She was a girl," Eddie said ruefully. "All of sixteen. There was another one, too. Eighteen. I guess I was trying to compensate for prom night at the luncheonette."

"And your wife did not want to become mired in kiddie litter," Leslie said smartly.

Eddie wore a startled grin. "That's one way of putting it," he said, smoothing the tablecloth with his palms to cover his shame.

Leslie was shocked by her own casual response, verging on the cynical. She tried to imagine him mounting a teenage girl. Her eyes meandered over his crotch and she could not take them off it. Ashamed, she did not know how to dispose of this grotesque attraction. She looked down, guiltily, at the table, as if watching for a cue about which fork to choose. The moonlight held her in a silvery crevice, far removed from earthly transgressions. She breathed a moment of eternity.

"Hi," Eddie said lightly, waving his hand in front of her face to bring her back.

Leslie seized on his improved mood. "But you see your other son?"

"Yes." Eddie effused: "My boy spends every summer

with me. It's part of the agreement that I get him for two months a year. He loves it here. He takes to the water like a fish. You should see him water-ski—on the one ski. He's a top-notch sailor too. The kid's amazing, a real natural athlete. Back home in Detroit he's captain of the football team—the first sophomore to make captain. Usually it's a senior heading it all up.''

"Terrific.''

Eddie smiled wistfully. "Did you get your whole interview, Miss Rittman?'' he joked.

Leslie thrust a closed fist toward his face as if it were a television microphone. "So, Mr. Harmon, what will you call your own restaurant? It will be a famous and popular place, I have no doubt.''

He blushed, which touched her. At the same time she understood how quickly resentments could grow out of confessions, particularly with men as unaccustomed as Eddie probably was to revealing themselves. Yet the island seemed to have the same draw as a bus depot or plane for spilling the guts.

Eddie cleared his throat and switched the topic away from himself. "*Your* work must be interesting,'' he said. "You probably go all over for stories.''

"Pretty much,'' Leslie replied modestly, worrying now about what he had done with the press card she coveted so much.

"What was the most exciting story?''

"Jimmy Hoffa.''

"You must be kidding?''

"Not at all,'' Leslie said. "In fact, I went to Detroit to do the interview.''

"Yeah?'' he said eagerly. "What'd you think of my hometown?''

Impishly, Leslie answered, "I think I may prefer Anlucia.''

He chuckled. "I won't take it personally." And then, turning serious, "I bet you go all over. Me, I'd just be glad to get the hell off this devil's island."

Leslie challenged: "You're free, white and over twenty."

"Wrong," he snapped. "I'm one jump ahead of a subpoena. The people I'm with wanted to get me out of the way to keep me from getting involved in a tax case. The feds were about to throw me in the slammer as a material witness. When the boss offered Anlucia, I figured it was a better deal. But it's going on two years now and I'm getting tired of cooling my heels down here."

He took a deep, exasperated breath and studied her fiercely, then pressed: "So why Hoffa?"

Relieved, she delivered an ode to the late labor leader, slipping almost reverently into his lingo. "He was one of those dese, dems and dose guys, but he knocked off a Harvard professor in a debate."

Eddie seemed to warm to her answer. "So how come a girl like you isn't married? I'd have thought, with all you've got going for you, the guys would be knocking down your door."

"Not exactly." She winced, remembering that she had just lost one of the only men who mattered in her life. The observation stabbed Leslie, and she forced herself to concentrate on the fascination she held for men like Eddie who, she suspected, saw a no-nonsense, pure quality about her, the detachment, wanting nothing, not even an ego prop.

"All night you look around at everything and everyone," he said softly, "except *me*. Why don't you look at me? Because I like you a lot. *I* look at *you*. Is this how you are with men?"

His attentiveness was like a caress. Leslie smiled, sweetly, and quivered. Eddie took her hand, squeezed it hard and swung it between their chairs.

Leslie could feel the envious stares of three women at the next table who appeared to be straining to hear what they were saying. With few eligible men to go around on the island, they sat with faces like clenched fists and drank Perrier and white wine. One of them ferreted inside a pocketbook stuffed with what looked like tissues and scraps of paper from three years ago, reminding Leslie of one of those debutante bag-ladies.

Eddie seemed unaware of them. The band was playing again. An old couple moved stiffly, their elbows taut and outstretched, across the dance floor. "Scrape, scrape," Eddie mimicked, making the same sound under the table.

She was horrified. Would a little squirming on her part, Leslie stewed, sufficiently amuse this man? Or did Eddie have other, trickier, contortions in mind?

He winked at her. Leslie did not like this type of eye movement, so duplicitous, she thought, as to be confused with a twitch. Her own eyes would never budge to synchronize with a point of humor or wisdom. There were almost no pure winks. "Do you want something else?" Eddie offered. "Or should we go?"

"Either way . . . whatever you prefer."

"Let's go, then," he said, "and cheer up."

Strolling back to the driveway, Eddie plucked a flower from a hibiscus bush and stuck it in her hair. Inside the car he turned the key forward and then, rolling it back, let his hand fall on the seat beside him. "I had a great evening," he murmured, staring straight ahead. "I can't remember having such a good time in a long while." He pressed her hand for a response. "How about you?"

"I had a lovely time, thank you." Leslie did not withdraw her hand directly, but sort of squiggled it free. She was feeling lethargic and propped herself up in the seat to keep from dozing. She opened the window for air.

Out of nowhere Eddie wondered aloud, "How come

you're still going away on vacations with your family?"

"I don't know." She shrugged. "Habit, I guess."

"Oh," he said. "How old are you?"

"Thirty," Leslie replied without hesitation. She never understood why people lied about their age. "What about you?"

"Thirty-eight going on twenty-two," Eddie laughed. "I still feel like a kid."

"Great."

Great what, Leslie wondered, suddenly remembering that she owed this man ten thousand dollars. She shuddered at her recollection of the broken arms and legs of the young man stuffed in the trunk of a Plymouth a year ago on the island. In the last twenty-four hours she felt she had aged ten years, her shoulders stooping from the weight of the casino debt and her face puffy from lack of sleep. They rode in silence, tense with the previous night between them.

Up ahead she saw the casino set on a barren hill surrounded by barbed wire. The car skidded over pebbles, unsettling Leslie, who clutched the armrest on her door.

The taxis were lined up outside the casino. It was close to ten, the peak arrival time, and casino regulars, some with wives and children in tow, were heading inside. Leslie felt comforted by the presence of other people.

Eddie nudged the car into a parking place away from the entrance. He started to hand Leslie her keys, but then closed them in his fist. "How about a brandy?" he said, shaking the keys like dice. "I'm not in the mood to go back to work right now."

"Okay," she said weakly.

As the car coasted down the hill, Eddie said casually, "Why don't we sit on my terrace? I'm the next hill over."

Now that she had already committed herself to a drink, there was no way to bow out gracefully. Was she crazy not to protest? She had never used men to get or to get out of things. It was an illusion, though, that Leslie was fiercely independent, always rejecting gifts and plane tickets from men who cared for her. "Don't accept presents," her father repeatedly warned, "or else you'll get owned." In the process she took from him, including this trip. That way she was beholden to no one else—no one but him. Now there was no chance of going to her father, and the situation was so impure that a few fast fucks might not be such a bad idea. But would Eddie settle?

The road to Eddie's place struggled upward through stubborn thickets of thorn and cactus. Patches of red soil peered, like bloodshot eyes, though lattice screens of acacia with their tough gnarled twigs and yellow blossoms. Wild cherries jostled with acacia bushes for survival among the outcrops of rock and eroded slope.

The house sat on a windy summit. It had the look of a design workshop, with Mediterranean tile floors, a rough cotton sofa and butcher-block table in the combined living-dining area, and two simple bedrooms. A bar unit on the terrace overlooked the sea. It was difficult to learn more about Eddie from the house, which was apparently leased. His personal effects seemed limited to a few paperback best sellers, including Mario Puzo's *Fools Die*, and a Frank Sinatra album that Leslie glimpsed on top of the stereo.

"I'm out of brandy," Eddie called out from the kitchen. "What else would you like?"

"I think I'd better stay with the rum punch," Leslie replied absently, "or better yet a Coca-Cola or some juice." She stood on the terrace and watched the shadowy outlines of what appeared to be little goats grazing in the moonlight.

Eddie came out with two rum punches, which he set on the ledge. He moved his face next to Leslie's to look at the view, with the twinkling Christmas lights in the town and the sea beyond. They both turned their heads at the exact moment, the corner of Eddie's mouth lightly brushing Leslie's lips. She pushed him away, and he drew her back, the press of his chest, wildly beating, against her.

"Please," Leslie murmured, "no."

Eddie let go. "Here"—his voice trembled—"I fixed you a drink."

Leslie took it out of his hand and said nothing.

"Look," Eddie stumbled, "I didn't mean to come on so strong. I hope I didn't surprise you."

"Oh, don't worry about it," Leslie said, hoping her forgiveness might keep him away, yet feeling pressure build inside her groin.

He touched Leslie's shoulders as though she were fragile. She felt she would cry from the tenderness. Slowly, Eddie turned her around to face him. "Oh," he moaned, "don't cry." He dried a tear with a few kisses on her cheek. Then he took her face in both hands and stroked it. She felt her whole body beginning to cave in to his touch. His lips wisped across hers softly, the kisses growing longer, his tongue rolling around her mouth. She liked the dryness of his kisses and the fact that he didn't slurp. She felt his prick grow hard, and now they were writhing against each other, the kisses becoming more impassioned and frantic.

Eddie took her hand, leading her into the bedroom with its floor-to-ceiling windows facing the sea. Desire pinned them to the bed, a huge platform. Eddie's hands stroked her legs, thighs, breasts, hiking her dress up to the shoulders. He sucked on one nipple, making it grow large and hard in his mouth, and twirled the other between his thumb and forefinger, then moved his hand down to her vagina, rotated his palm lightly over it and, spreading its lips, stroked it like the petals of a velvety flower, his fingers moving in and out of her. Leslie unzipped his pants and caressed his penis, then matched her genitals against his in a grinding motion. She lay on her back now, no longer able to wait, and guided his penis inside her. He moved deeply, in and out, sucking up the darkness in her belly, thrusting with ferocity as she tickled his back and neck, then scratched as he shoved it so hard inside her, screaming as she floated, her whole body tingling, off the bed. Her mouth was completely dry, and her ears were ringing.

They lay still a few minutes, their entwined bodies damp and sticky. Each time they tried to get up they fell into another embrace, pulling the sheets tightly to draw themselves even closer. Eddie lifted his arm out from under her to unkink it. She saw it was already eleven-thirty on the clock by the telephone.

"Oh, my God," Leslie said, "I've got to get the car back."

Eddie rose first, sitting up in bed and fondling her breasts. "What do you prefer—tits or breasts?"

"Why?"

"For future reference." He smiled, letting the breast, sore and swollen from sex, roll out of his palm as he planted a kiss on her forehead. "Thanks."

"Do you mind if I take a quick shower?"

"No, go ahead. There's a clean towel on the rack."

She picked through their clothes, tangled in the sheets, and gathered up her own, taking them into the bathroom. Her body felt silky and soft from his touch as she soaped her arms and legs. She turned on the cold water to snap herself awake. For some reason she thought of Marc, who sang arias in the shower. He had been her best lover and also one of the most powerful men in his field. Their affair had been perfect, with a beginning, middle and end. He had offered her help with a job search. Leslie rejected the offer: "If I did this, then I would violate the whole reason I was with you in the first place."

Hurriedly climbing into her underpants and slipping on her bra and caftan, Leslie emerged from the bathroom.

Eddie was already dressed for work, in a black tuxedo with a blue ruffled shirt. He stood with his back to her, adjusting his cufflinks.

"Eddie," she began, "I don't want you to think I'm not going to pay you. It wouldn't be right. I'll get you the money, but I may need a few extra days until I'm back in the city and can arrange for it."

There was a knock at the door. "Forget the money," Eddie snapped as he went to answer it. She heard a male voice: "I got in a few hours ago and kept calling. Am I interrupting anything?"

"Nothing," Eddie said, and led his visitor back into the bedroom. "This is Vince." The man, broad-shouldered, with shiny black hair and a greenish slack to his face, surveyed the rumpled sheets and grinned at Leslie. He sniffed the room like a bloodhound, the smell of sex that permeated it. She looked at Eddie to rescue her from this humiliation. He raised his brow disdainfully and rolled a cigar around his mouth, wetting the tip of it by biting down on it, then held it up to inspect and light. The smoke nauseated her.

Leslie felt as if she had been standing at bay for hours. She was afraid to budge an inch, for fear of making a wrong move. She held her breath and listened to thick droplets of rain splatter the ground, growing into a downpour, the rain thrashing the roof and the lights flickering. The wind cracked the palm fronds that scratched the side of the house. Leslie strained to listen for the storm to abate. If the rain kept up at this force, the road would be a mudslide, unnegotiable, trapping her until the midday sun might mold the earth back together. She concentrated on stopping the tropical storm, its ferocity winding down, longer spaces between the raindrops, then just the fall-out of water dripping off the roof and shrubbery. It stopped, as abruptly as it had started.

"Let's go out on the terrace," Eddie said to his visitor. He looked back at Leslie. "You, too," he barked.

He wiped the chairs dry and went inside to fix drinks. Except for crickets sawing the trees, the night was totally still. She waited for a cue from Vince, but he only slumped deeper into his seat and stared at her.

Eddie returned and shoved a rum punch into Leslie's hand.

"No, thanks," she begged off. "I'm exhausted. I think I should leave you two gentlemen alone."

"Where the hell do you think you're going?" Eddie snarled. "You sit!" He was Casino Eddie again. The mood-swing chilled her like an ice cube down the front of her dress. Then, turning his back, he announced, "She can sleep late. She's on vacation. A lucky girl. The ole man picks up the tab for the whole family."

"Yeah," Vince said eagerly, leaning into the remark.

"She's a reporter," Eddie sniffed. "You don't think she could afford the Sandy Cove on her own."

Vince shoved his hands in front of his body in mock disgust. "You know I ain't crazy about these reporters," he cracked.

"She's a different story," Eddie said coolly. "I own a piece of her."

Though Vince seemed to be enjoying his voyeuristic corner in this triangle, he was starting to cave in to fatigue, twice falling backward in the chair before getting out of it. "I think"—he yawned—"I'm too tired to fuck the reporter. I'll just hit the sack."

"There are fresh towels on the bathroom rack," Eddie called after him cheerily. "See you in the morning." He glared over a cigar at Leslie while trying to revive it with several futile clicks of a beveled gold lighter.

"I'm going to pay you," Leslie wailed.

"Get outta here," he mocked. "You haven't got that kind of money."

"I'll get it."

"You don't think I'd let your kind sign for all those hard-luck chips if I was worried."

"Then why did you?"

"Guess."

"What on earth are you talking about?" she pleaded.

He paused, puffing hard on the cigar to get it going. Curls of smoke cast a grayish tint on the lightly tanned face. The Midwestern boyishness seemed submerged now in the sheen of a gangster tuxedo that did not fit him. It was almost a drag scene, with Eddie putting on a false face, his blue eyes a glint, the mouth a tight slit. "Where the hell would you come by that kind of cash?" he sputtered angrily. "Oh, yes, your daddy. But I don't need his bread. I could cover the ten grand on the books any day of the week. I just want your ole man to do his job and throw out that stale case."

"My father," she loudly protested, "would never do anything crooked. Not for me, not for you or anyone else! Nobody! No way!"

"Crooked," Eddie sniffed. "What do you think he's been doing for the last two years? What's so straight about sitting on a tax case for two years like a mother hen, keeping it warm for the U.S. attorney who has no case and never had one. If it had been my people's lawyers stalling for witnesses, he would have dumped them out on their asses a long time ago."

"I owe you the money," Leslie seethed, "and I'm going to pay you, and I wouldn't touch your crooked mess with a ten-foot pole."

Eddie slammed the wall just below the patio light, flipped his hand over and inspected the dead black insects stuck to his palm. "Who the hell are you to get so indignant?" he shouted. "Awhile ago you were Miss Liberty, shooting your mouth off about the Sixth Amendment. Now, when your old man's involved, you're singing another tune. And who told you to piss away money that you didn't have in the first place?"

Leslie could feel the blotches of red anger on her face draining into a sickly green. "Then you—oh no! You set me up?"

"You got it."

"You're the missing witness," she accused, "and you're hiding out here."

"I didn't do anything wrong," he taunted. "What was I supposed to do, hang around until they served me with papers? This isn't Russia. It's a free country. I can go anywhere I want or the boss tells me. You better talk to your old man, or else he's going to have worse news."

"No," she screamed.

"What do you mean, 'No'?" he said, menace in his tone. "How would he like to see a little item in the gossips? 'A certain federal court judge's daughter barely missed a contract on her life in Anlucia after dropping ten grand one night at the casino there. . . .' He ain't going to smell like a rose."

"No, no, no!" Leslie said, pounding the armrests of her chair.

"I know one thing," he thundered, "I'm getting the hell off this lousy island. And your daddy's my ticket to freedom. And one more thing—*you're* not getting out of here unless you do what I tell you!"

Eddie reached into his trouser pocket and took out the car keys, dangling them before her, then pulling them back. Leslie grabbed his arm angrily, her fingernails digging into him as he tried to wrench himself free. He jerked his arm away and inspected the pinkish scrapes on his wrist. He dropped the keys on the floor and pushed her to the ground to pick them up.

"Now get out of here," he hissed. "Get the hell out of here, you little whore. Go on—you piece of New York shit. Bitch."

11

Anyone could tell that she no longer belonged—to the tropical sun, cool breeze off the sea and the family holiday scene. Leslie was too anxious, looking over her shoulder, marking time on the beach in her tennis clothes.

"Leslie," her mother implored, "put on a bathing suit. It's just too hot to sit like this."

"No, I'd rather not. I'm more comfortable this way."

Quite inadvertently, Jason came to her defense. "Are you ready for the tennis tournament?" he challenged, staring impassively at Leslie and sniffing twice. "I left you a note about it. I'm going to whip your ass. I signed you up for it. And I'm about to expose you to an ignominious defeat right after lunch."

"Don't bet on it." Leslie sighed. She struggled to keep up the appearance of the combative spirit encouraged by the family, but was feeling too burned out to muster even the commitment needed to become a sore loser.

Rebecca, stretching sleep out of her body on the next mat, piped up, "You should have come with us last night. Where were you anyway? We all won."

"What?" Leslie started, closing her eyes to hide the panic in them.

"At the casino," Rebecca said cheerily, her inquiry about Leslie's whereabouts the night before lost in her enthusiastic replay of the evening. "I won fifty dollars. Mommy and Daddy made over two hundred. Jason, the cheapskate, only bet ten dollars and came away with about two."

Leslie feigned sleep, but was shaken fully awake by Holly's loud voice, blotting out a wave that thrashed the shore and sucked up sand under the legs of the chaise longues. Everyone jumped up to pull back from the water line. Whenever her sister-in-law tried to make a point, as she was now doing in a discussion with Leslie's father about oil prices, she raised her voice, reminding Leslie of tourists who shout in English at Parisian taxi drivers on the theory that the insistence of their speech, landing on every syllable, might overcome the language barrier. Holly's talk produced in Leslie the effect of a migraine. She wanted to pummel Holly's head with pillows to shut it out.

Rebecca was also annoyed. Their sister-in-law, though well informed, seemed too intellectually striving, somehow re-creating the tension they recognized in their own conversations with their father. Jason looked approvingly at his wife, his expression a fusion of a smile and a squint.

"You should have seen Holly," Rebecca sniped. "I thought she was only scared of the water, bugs and strangers. She was frightened to gamble."

Leslie grimaced at her sister-in-law. "Look," she cracked, "Holly got over her fear of using an escargot fork, so she can conquer the gambling too. Then she'll probably get real sick from both."

She wondered now if Holly, who did not seem to notice herself shouting, might in fact be a little hard of hearing. Epiphanies that might lead to impassioned speech did not come upon people like Holly. Nor was she someone capable of recognizing or rising to them. There was a copper quality to Holly's intelligence, lots of facts and few deeply felt moments; totally inured was she, even now, to the golden tenor of the sea, the sun bellydancing inside the waves. Such a mind was a violation of the hallucinatory way in which Leslie saw things even as a child. Her parents' approval of Holly's tidy mind, with no stray cilia on the brain cells, was an infuriating reminder of how they had sought to unscramble Leslie's consciousness, bundling her off to the shrink as though she were going to the dentist to have a toothed pulled. What was the difference, anyway? Dr. Abraham Kimmel, her fourth and current psychoanalyst, tried to yank out of her the sorrow and rage which, though unhealed wounds, were yet the psychic wellspring from which she could draw reserves of imagination, something she kept like a candle by her bed in the dark. She felt straitjacketed in Kimmel's office, filled with cactus plants, *his* penis envy, and a tropical aquarium designed to trap the life of the mind and a few goldfish. Actually she found him to be a pain in the kazoo, not at all cool, really dreary, a big lump, about as exciting as a sigh on the stage . . . um, uh-huh, um, um, um, a drone.

At the moment she needed a fumigator, not a shrink, to expunge Eddie's odor, a mixture of cologne and cigar smoke gone slightly stale since the previous night, from her body. Bile was rising in her throat. She churned up saliva to dilute its acrid taste. She cradled her arms to comfort herself. The lotion felt gooey, and her tan now seemed like a creeping stain, soiling and muddying her. She got up and walked into the sea to splash water on her face and arms. Thoughts of Eddie pinched her mind. What a fool she had been to think he was going to give her a break. Tiny fish snaked around her foot, and she flicked her ankle to kick them away, banishing the memory of Eddie, the way he shed skins like some amphibious creature, the admiring glow on his face suddenly turning cruel and hateful.

As the water slithered over Leslie, she remembered the humiliation of her first sexual experience with Emil, an older man. At the moment of penetration, Leslie, too dry to accept his penis, screamed from the pain, jumped out of bed and put her clothes back on. She had been too embarrassed to suggest Vaseline for fear of appearing too mechanical. Emil, just divorced by a wife fifteen years younger, recommended that Leslie loosen up in the sea by his private beach on the island. The remedy did not work. He was furious. His penis was limp. He had expected Leslie to be his raft, holding up his organ, when it would have taken a bicycle pump to do the job. Leslie spent the next few weeks blushing at his loss of grace.

She was poked to attention by Cynthia, her favorite of the women who peddled beads and handmade dresses on the beach. Robust, and if she had not been well into her fifties, she might have given the impression of being pregnant. Her narrow black eyes hinted of voodoo. She followed Leslie back to her place on the beach. "Leslie," she said, "I be look for you. Glad to hav you bahk. I want to tank you for dah radio."

Leslie's mother turned away sullenly and pulled her pocketbook onto her lap. Sensing the mood, Cynthia stuffed the dresses already laid out on a nearby mat back into a large straw bag and, without another word, walked off, her bright print dress, like a dashiki, merging with the carnival of colors worn by her cohorts.

With Cynthia out of hearing range, Leslie's mother scolded, "Which radio did you give her? You want to be a sucker. She's just using you. If your father and I didn't pay

161

for these trips, you couldn't afford to be so generous."

"It's only a radio"—her father defended her—"Don't make a federal case out of it, Sarah."

Encouraged by his defense, Leslie became enthusiastic. "I really like Cynthia. She's very smart and independent. She told me she would rather do this than be a waitress at the hotels. 'Dis way I be my own boss.'"

Her father looked oddly at Leslie. "Don't get carried away with one of your romantic fantasies," he cautioned. "She's a peddler, not an entrepreneur."

"That depends on your definition."

A waitress interrupted him. "Dere's a long-distance call for you, sir."

Jason took over where his father left off. "Leslie," he chuckled, "I wouldn't count on Cynthia's business acumen to bail out Chrysler. She's a con artist."

"What are you talking about?" Leslie shot back. "You little snob!"

Their mother huffed. "She's a user."

"A userer?" Leslie taunted.

"I said user!"

"Oh." Leslie smirked, reminded of how much 'gelt'—Yiddish for money, and one of the few words her mother knew in the old language—sounded like guilt.

User, usurer; gelt, guilt.

"Mom," Rebecca wailed, "Cynthia is really smart. I've talked to her."

Whenever Rebecca tried to defend a position, a stern look crossed her face, insistence hardening the delicate sensibility Leslie treasured in her sister and recognized as something that went far beyond her feminine charms, to the way she stroked a child's head or lightly turned pages of writing Leslie might show her.

Jason now had a visitor, an islander in cutoff jeans and a

torn T-shirt. "What time, mahn?" He grinned, a sooty smile forming between his lips.

"Five?" Jason said cryptically.

"Okay, mahn." He yawned, rubbing his bloodshot eyes. "Twill be twenty dollars. You wan to pay me now or latah?"

"I'll give it to you then," Jason stated, almost as a warning. Apparently he knew the old I'll-leave-it-under-a-rock trick, wherein some sucker pays the money up front and nearly gets a hernia lifting the rock, only to find the stash missing and hear the next day that someone got there first.

"Okay, mahn," he said, spinning on his bare heels over the sand and weaving his way down the beach.

"He sure looks like some bum," their mother commented.

No one argued with her description.

"His name is Wenty." Jason fidgeted. "Short for Wentworth."

"Some name," their mother remarked critically, a stab at a perception of which she could not grab hold.

"He's in charge of horseback riding," Jason explained. "He's not going to dress up when he works in the bar in this heat."

"He *rides*?" Sarah Rittman said incredulously. "He can hardly stand."

Rebecca, burying a giggle inside the crease of a paperback book, chimed in: "He's supposed to be terrific."

"How would you know?" their mother inquired of Rebecca. "You don't even ride."

"I have my connections on the island," she said, then broke into a refrain from the Gladys Knight and the Pips hit song about grapevine.

"What do I know?" Their mother shrugged. She reached

into her pocketbook, pulled out a twenty-dollar bill and handed it to Jason.

"It's okay," he said, folding the fingers of her hand to make it impossible for her to release the bill. "I can afford it."

"Take it," she demanded. "The money won't make any difference in your father's or my life. I have plenty."

"That's not the point," Jason said weakly, unconvincingly.

The little crook, Leslie fumed, the model son, deliberate and self-serving in his trickeries, something that embittered Leslie, who had tried to be a good daughter, getting all A's through school and working hard, not hurting or making a fool of people or ending up in jail overnight for smoking pot. The ruination Leslie made of her life and the family in the casino had been wholly unpremeditated. Jason, with his damn Ph.D., was as much a plotter as a plodder.

A wind carried the twenty-dollar bill across the sand. Jason scrambled to pull it in, stashing the money under his beach mat.

"Don't make a big deal out of this," Sarah declared. "Now will one of you please go and see where your father is. He should tell that law clerk he's on vacation. He doesn't have to get calls here."

"I'll go," Leslie volunteered, the dutiful daughter.

"And see our tickets are confirmed," Sarah fussed.

Dashing through the lobby, she popped her head into the hotel conference room and caught her father's eye. He was jotting notes on a yellow legal pad, his security blanket, and he held up a pencil to tell her to wait a minute—which stretched into fifteen. Her father could retire and live comfortably the rest of his life. With the pressure on Leslie to come up with ten thousand, she could not understand why he did not get out while he was ahead. Long before the judgeship, he could have well afforded to drop the smaller clients and just keep open the large accounts. But the nickel-and-dime people were the chips he started with and wisely held on to over the years. He still carried on in a frenzied way inside his judicial chambers, his desk over-flowing with tall stacks of legal files and memos, rather than at the gambling tables. Theodore Rittman, his daughter thought proudly, was a survivor, not a self-destructor.

Jason came through the doorway where Leslie stood guard. She looked past her brother's shoulder for a sudden appearance by Casino Eddie, as their father signaled that he would be a few more minutes.

"This is insanity," Jason whispered tensely. "Why does he do it?"

"Because he needs to support his children's marijuana habit."

"It wasn't my fault," Jason protested shamelessly. "You saw the way Mommy kept pushing the money at me."

"Yeah," Leslie grunted, "and your intense resistance."

Wincing at her father, still on the phone after ten more minutes had passed, Leslie shrugged and told her brother, "You wait . . . I give up."

Inside the lobby, next to the front desk, Leslie saw that the tennis and sailing boutique was open. It had been shut, with black wrought-iron gates, until now. A sporting goods store was her Bloomingdale's. Rooms with wall-to-wall tennis balls were like a womb to her. She liked to look at all the new equipment and then try the grip of several rackets, shaking them defiantly and making a whipping sound. If she ever got married, she would probably register at Herman's World of Sporting Goods in New York for such gifts as two hundred cans of tennis balls, thirty Lacoste shirts, six sweat suits and the latest in Fiberglas snow skis.

In the boutique Leslie inspected her eyebrows in a mir-ror. Whenever she felt her life in disarray she treated her-self to a manicure and eyebrow wax.

"They look fine," said a woman, peering over Leslie's shoulder in the mirror.

The directness was riveting and Leslie spun around to study her further. The voice was pure as a glass of distilled water. "Are you a singer?"

"Yes," the woman said. "How did you know?"

"You have a lovely voice."

"How kind of you to say so." She beamed. "What do you do?"

"I'm a writer for *You* magazine."

"Don't tell me . . . I'll bet *you're* Leslie Rittman," she said joyously. "I was just reading your article on the beach yesterday and thought it was so excellent I showed it to someone who said you were here. What a coincidence. I was saying I wanted to meet you."

"Thanks." Leslie rejoiced. "Thanks." The boutique became a blur. She could not see beyond the compliment, the first since the start of the family holiday.

The singer extended her hand. "Hi, I'm Joanna Rowe." The handshake, eager and sturdy without being a bone-crusher, pleased Leslie.

The cashier, a plump islander in an orange polka-dot dress, with an outsized imitation Gucci bag practically dragging her arm to the floor, breezed absently into the shop.

"Good," Leslie greeted her, "you're back." She remembered with shame now that she had no purchases to speak of nor the money to make any, having spent every last cent at the casino.

"I be at dah strike meeting and den we have a tea break," she explained. "We may be hav picket tomorrow." Her nostrils, wide like those on African carvings, flared proudly.

Joanna nodded as if siding with her. There was no trace of ridicule at the corners of her mouth. She set a bottle of

Evian water and a tortoise-shell barrette on the counter. Certain women, Leslie thought, could carry off ponytails, which often even enhanced their beauty and revealed delicate ears.

The cashier opened her palm, holding it up like a clipboard. On it was scribbled a price list in blue ink, fading from perspiration and nearly illegible. "Dat twill be two dollars and forty cents," she read, then collected the money, figured the change on an enormous calculator and handed it over.

"What's your name?" Leslie inquired in a friendly tone.

"Daisy May."

"What a lovely name. I think maybe I'll steal it if you don't mind."

Daisy May giggled. "You both be hav a good day."

Leslie waited for a cue about lunch or a drink from Joanna, whose sexy laugh gave her goose bumps. "I have to rehearse," Joanna announced, "and then try to get in a nap."

"How about if I come along and listen," Leslie prodded. "Everyone needs feedback."

Joanna begged off. "I need to work alone. But I'll sound you out after the show tonight."

"Sure." Leslie shrugged. "See you later."

She watched as Joanna walked away, wanting to run after her, as if chasing parts missing inside herself. Gorgeous, smart, charming and a singer to boot—Joanna Rowe was whole. But Leslie hardly knew her. Maybe there was nothing more to this woman than what she was reading into her. No wonder Pin the Tail on the Donkey was a child's game. Leslie remembered how the blindfolded kids all groped for a place on the paper donkey, taped to a wall, to stick the pin. Perhaps she fastened her needs on someone else in the same way.

She walked dejectedly back to the beach. Her father was

playing with a child who looked to be about five. Bending his pinky inside his palm, her father cried out, "My finger is missing."

The boy grabbed hold of the hand, insisting Leslie's father was wrong. Then he skittered around the chaise longue and began to dig up sand in search of the missing finger.

"I found it, I found it," her father chanted. "It was on my lap all this time."

The boy wagged his head in total amazement. In the next moment he said boldly, "It was on your hand the whole time." Nonetheless, he seemed quite relieved to see five digits on her father's right hand. "Okay, bye," he said, still slightly confused.

Leslie's father had been a wonderful storyteller, inventing all manner of conversations with the family pets at home to write her about in summer camp letters. A favorite game of his was to fill up the coin box of a pay phone with quarters, pull down on it and then watch the money cascade out of it. Somehow none of his children could produce the same results—to this day. Until her teens Leslie had enjoyed his company, whether playing catch under the big old apple tree in the backyard or knowing he watched as she took a spin on a merry-go-round or around an ice-skating rink. He became overwhelmed later on with work that made him wealthy and distant, spending Sundays at the office, shutting the front door of the house quietly and starting up the car slowly as he idled it out of the driveway, just as Leslie tiptoed past his cottage on the way back from the casino— quiet spaces of guilt.

Jason interrupted her musings. "You better get something to eat," he said. "The tournament is soon."

"I'd rather play on an empty stomach," Leslie said, and repaired to her room to fetch her racket and put on socks. She opened the door to the patio and found her sneakers.

She always left them outside to air overnight. She shuffled into the shoes. Her right toe bumped up against what felt like a small stone. She kicked off the shoe and bent down to shake it out. A wooden disk fell out of the shoe and rolled onto the beach. Leslie picked it out of the sand. It was a gambling chip and on its face in block letters was IOU. Smelly sneakers might deter other foes. But not Eddie. He was on her track. There was no running away. Her legs wobbled, and she crouched into an agonizing deep knee bend, suddenly landing on her backside. The chip stuck to her palm, and she rubbed it into the sand. Leslie sat there on the steamy patio, caught in the dizzying shimmer of the day's heat that deprived her momentarily of air to breathe. At the first hint of a wind she got up, cautiously, and began making her way to the tennis courts.

She was the first to arrive at the match. A middle-aged couple was on the court. The woman tapped the ball repeatedly into the net while her husband, not much better, kept up the illusion that he was hitting it softly to her. Occasionally he barked instructions at her.

"Don't swat at it. Keep your eye on the ball. Stand sideways."

And the wife, pleading coyly, answered, "Irv, I'm trying."

Leslie loved the game, predicated on talent and drive. There was a cleanness and fairness to it. Either a player could stroke the ball or not. Right there, on court, was the direct verdict. If a wind intruded, carrying the ball out of bounds, both players were pitted equally against the odds, no stacked decks. The strength of her game was one certainty in Leslie's life. No one could question it or tear it down.

The players were starting to arrive, some twenty in all, gathering around a card table with a pitcher of lemonade on it.

"Okay, folks," the Texan tennis pro said in her best camp counselor voice, "we'll be starting in ten minutes."

She shook up a hat with numbers on stubs of colored paper and passed it around. One man stuffed his hand into it like a kid with a cookie jar. The only other woman player, a fiftyish former ski and tennis champion in her native Hungary, clawed the pieces of paper with her long cherry-colored fingernails, drawing two stubs by accident, putting them back and picking again. Leslie had observed her cheating on line calls and then defending them in the stern, gutteral voice of a Nazi drill sergeant. Closing her eyes and turning her head away from the hat, Leslie drew a number. It was an automatic response, a test of truthfulness from her childhood.

She saw her number was the same one as Jason pulled. They would play against each other in the first round. But his braggadocio was fast crumbling. "Don't give me any points," Jason warned, as if conceding defeat.

They rallied for a few minutes, long enough for her to see that Jason's game was off. Nevertheless, she felt proud watching her baby brother, tucked into his tennis whites, grapple with the game. Leslie had taught Jason, a heretofore hopeless athlete, to play, and in recent times he had occasionally beaten her.

Now Jason wanted to win so badly that he was beating himself. He whacked the ball for winners and lost three consecutive games.

"Patience," Leslie called out to him. "Keep the ball in play. Wait for a winner."

In the fifth game Jason punched three straight serves out of the box, to make the score 5–0, in her favor. Leslie then compounded the injury by acing him twice, moving her two points away from taking the set. Jason, shaking his head wildly, chastised himself. "Idiot, jerk," he said, slapping his forehead.

Winding up her right arm in a huge arc, as a prelude to a wallop of a serve, Leslie watched him retreat to a position behind the baseline in order to retrieve what promised to be a deep ball. Then she tapped the ball lightly, dropping it an inch or two from the net in the serving box on his side, forcing Jason to run clear across the court to return the serve. He overran it, adding an almost comical overtone to the game. Jason always fell for this ploy, cursing himself a second later. He berated himself now as he waited to kill her next serve. He overshot it and blew the set.

In one motion he put his racket back in its cover and walked hurriedly away from the defeat.

Rushing to catch up with him, Leslie clutched his arm and said, "Sorry, Jason. I don't know how it happened so fast. You're a fine player. You beat yourself. I didn't do it."

He peered at her apology through wire-rimmed eyeglasses misted with disappointment. Dismissing her apology, he challenged, "Then why was the score six-love? You won it fair and square."

"Okay." She pulled back, slightly ashamed now about tricking him on that short serve. Maybe she should have saved it for their home court.

Guiltily, she walked over to the tournament scorer and whispered the match result, penciled into a square box on a large sheet of cardboard. Moving up the ladder of players, Leslie mopped the Hungarian monster off the court in another shutout to gain a place in the finals. The woman's ungenerous spirit about dubious calls shot adrenaline through Leslie's will to win.

Now most of the original players gathered around the pro to watch the final bout. The mood as they arranged themselves in the bleachers was more relief at not having to endure another set under the blazing sun than disappointment at losing.

"You're one helluva player," a doctor who came to

Sandy Cove year after year told Leslie. "You just get better and better."

She studied her opponent, his muscles tensed inside strong, golden-tanned legs, and figured him for first singles on his college team. Unsure whether she could outlast him, Leslie ransacked her brain for a goal that might force victory on her. Hearing from Adam? Getting a book published? Ten thousand prize money to cancel her debt? She settled on the last option, using it like a whip to move a horse into a gallop. With that sum riding on the match Leslie would keep herself in the running, overtaking the young colt.

They rallied a few minutes, long enough for Leslie to devise a strategy. Mix up the shots, whack the ball and then let up, plunk down a hundred-dollar chip and then pull back with twenty-five on the next. To show all her cards in a consistent manner would give him a decided advantage, would allow him to string her along, giving up a point, a bet here and there, but he would know when to knock her off balance and would eventually clean up. They shook hands and wished each other luck.

With the exception of his parents, the spectators rooted for Leslie to win, turning their admiration on this thirty-year-old woman with the drive to face a boy at least ten years younger. Leslie felt she did not deserve this adulation; didn't she have another identity as a gambler? "Isn't that the woman we saw in the casino?" she thought she heard a woman ask her husband, who shooed away the question: "No . . . now let me watch the match." Leslie connected hard with the ball, the whack of the serve blotting out her accuser's voice, and then struggled to concentrate on the return, which touched the white canvas tape and then curled back on her opponent's side. She won the first point, eventually gaining the game.

His serve was like a tornado, a real twister, and Leslie

held out her racket in self-defense. Miraculously, it worked. There was enough power in his serve to send the ball over the net and back again. Had Leslie attempted to hit the ball instead of fend it off, she would have knocked it out of bounds. Ill prepared for her timid response, he killed the return of service with equal ferocity, sending the ball over her head and way out of the court.

"Home run," Leslie cheered, to a chorus of laughs.

Now she was taking his service, too, crucial to clinching the set and tournament. The score was 4–2, in her favor, two games away from claiming the prize money. She started to tire. Her tennis clothes, soaked with sweat, put a chill in her body in the waning afternoon. Ten more points, at a thousand a shot, was all it would take. Leslie grabbed hold of herself, varying her shots, slicing the ball, slamming it, hitting it at his feet, putting a spin on it, carrying it away from him and, finally, to victory.

She could barely stand up. Her head hung low as she tried to get a second wind. Through a haze of exhaustion she observed a blur of bodies moving about the bleachers. Her head stayed down, dragged by instinct, but she felt a stare shooting black darts her way. She studied the strings of her racket and pressed her fingers against them as if vibrating a cello. Yet there was this urge to face the intruder. She looked up: Eddie's face, a fuzzy image, zoomed into focus. He stared at her a second, just long enough to make contact and shatter her victory. She shut her eyes to blot him out. When she opened them, he was gone.

The tennis pro held up a trophy in her hands, skin crinkled from the tropical sun, and motioned Leslie to join her in front of the card table. "Good going," she cheered. "A great win. Right, folks?" Everyone clapped dutifully. She reached down to lift a can of tennis balls which she also presented to Leslie.

"Thanks," Leslie said, walking away from the table.

"Whoa," the pro called out. "We've got something else for you."

"What?" Leslie muttered.

The pro handed her a needlepoint racket cover. Leslie unzipped it as she trudged back to the room. She was knocked out, but half-enjoyed the sensation. What felt like a pin pricked her finger as she swished her hand inside the case. She did not like what she felt, a round chip with a scrap of paper pinned to it. She unfastened the note and read, "Did you talk to Daddy yet?" She heard footsteps gaining on her on the concrete walk. Leslie kept up the same stride, hoping that inattention might call him off. The body moved closer, and she could feel his breath on her neck. Then came a poke, tentative, yet forceful, in her back.

"What!" Leslie's shriek caused the family, watching the fading twilight on the beach, to look up in her direction.

Before her stood the boy whom she had just defeated in the match. "I'm sorry if I scared you," he said, stroking his racket strings to hide what seemed like a developing crush on Leslie.

"It's okay." Leslie shrugged, trying to shake off a nervousness that left her feeling numb.

"I just wanted to tell you how much I admire your game," he said. "You're really great."

"Thanks."

"I mean it," he said earnestly. "Maybe we could play some tomorrow or the day after. You could give me a few pointers."

"Sure," Leslie replied, and added, "Do you like to gamble?"

"I've never tried it," he said shyly. "My parents said they might take me one night."

Glad to unload the chip, which she saw was worth twenty-five dollars, Leslie attempted to comfort him. "You played very well. No one likes to lose. Here, take the chip and have a good time." She crumpled the note in her hand, the message fading from the sweat and leaving blue ink on her palm.

"Thanks," he said. "By the way, my name is Stephen."

She gave him an affectionate swat on the shoulder with her racket, a way of atoning for the drubbing she had meted out earlier to her brother. Leslie decided to join the family on the beach rather than return to her cottage alone. The sun was melting into a quarter moon.

"Where's Jason?" she greeted them.

"I sent him to check the reservations home," her mother said.

"Again," Leslie said in an exasperated tone. "I already did it this morning. Christ!"

"We're leaving the day after tomorrow," her mother reminded, adding self-righteously, "You'll be glad when you see all the people waiting on line without flights."

"It's a bore," Leslie snapped. She shivered from her damp body.

"Leslie," her father said, "you're blue. Here's my shirt. Cover up."

In the distance a frog-shaped rock sat, with stubbles of grass on its back, in the middle of the sea. Leslie watched the water slither and slide over it, almost burying it. A mammoth wave whacked the rock, for the moment covering it with foam, smothering it from view. Then the water receded, peeled back, the rock rising up ineluctably, immutable as her father's values.

Deep inside herself, Leslie knew he would give her his skin if it meant saving her, but at the moment she could not even accept the shirt off his back.

12

Leslie navigated her way to the bar by red lanterns strapped to every other palm tree. A cocktail, she felt, would be the perfect antidote to the burn on her face and the charley horse that threatened to settle into her muscles. The effect of a hot shower and baby powder sprinkled on her chest was already starting to wear off. Through the window of one cottage she saw an old couple, their heads propped against pillows in a coffinlike pose, reading. The curtains in her parents' room were drawn, but she made out their silhouettes, busily arranging themselves for dinner.

"Wait," someone called out in the darkness. "I'll walk with you." The voice belonged to Jason, who was crushing out a joint in the damp sand and moving hurriedly toward her. "Congratulations on the match."

"Oh," Leslie shrugged, "it was nothing."

Why was she always minimizing her triumphs? Jason had not even bothered to stick around for her win. Nor had any other family members shown up to cheer her on. They only seemed to rally around at times of sickness or failure. At Friday night dinners their father paused to consider all their wrongdoings, five demerits for a bad report card and half a point for a pimple. Then he totaled up the score and in the privacy of his mind proclaimed the underdog of the week. Each of the children prayed that he or she would not become the target of his excoriation. If one of them had a triumph, however small, that would move him or her up the ladder, which meant that someone else was dangerously close to the bottom rung. It was not that they did not wish each other well; it was more a matter of self-preservation.

In the bar Jason claimed the only seat, next to his wife, leaving Leslie to stand over the small table. A man with a scrawny beard, skinny arms and veiny hands slouched in a wicker chair with a fanlike back that enhanced his vampire image. "Is this the sister who works for *You*? he groused.

She intercepted his hostility with an effusive handshake. "Hi, I'm Leslie Rittman. Pleased to meet you."

Turning away, she was glad to see Joanna beckoning her to a table at the far end of the bar. The man beside Joanna was the same fellow Leslie had seen the night the family checked into the hotel. He had been at the front desk frantically trying to put through a call to New York while his daughter, vying for his attention, clicked the heels of her Mary Janes.

"Hi," he said cheerfully. "I'm Bernie Cohen."

His Bermuda shorts threatened to explode if he breathed too deeply. He had whiskerlike hairs on his sallow-tanned legs. His face was hot-red with strands of Aramis-scented perspiration. A caricature of what Bernie probably perceived to be style, he did not offend in any way, but just managed to miss. She imagined that his apartment in the East Eighties or on Central Park West had whites, wood and plenty of plants under track lights, a certain cleanliness of space and design favored by the recently divorced bachelor-about-town. What with alimony, child support and expensive dates, Leslie figured, he could only afford the maid once a week, on the day he feverishly entertained his daughter at the zoo. She wondered why Joanna would spend a second in his company.

Bernie was forthcoming with an explanation. "I take it you two know each other," he said. "I was just telling Joanna that when she's in New York promoting an album, she should give a yell and come on one of my programs."

"Which one?" Leslie asked.

"The Sally Henry Show," he replied with great self-importance. "I'm head of O and O."

"O and O?" she said with a snicker. "Sounds like a bug spray."

"Owned and Operated stations," Bernie said, flicking his cigar to punctuate the title. "Network."

His glibness was testimony to the fast-talking world of television that traded on such abbreviations, and which also characterized the superficial emotions and intellect of some of the people in the industry.

Leslie suddenly remembered how much she dreaded returning in three days to her office with the hermetically sealed windows. To get from the lobby to the twenty-fourth floor of the magazine she had to switch at eighteen, something like changing in Chicago for Los Angeles, but she always had an ineffable sense of going nowhere in the corporate maze. In Disbursing on twenty-eight they did not have imagination enough to vary the colors of the damn paycheck, which never seemed to expand either. But now that she had graduated to the Big Time, Leslie thought pathetically, Casino Eddie might just put through a call to the magazine to create a few unpleasant ripples in Ms. Rittman's career. Not wanting a degenerate gambler on the masthead, the editor might try to ease her out.

Bernie offered her a drink. "What will you have?"

"A rum punch."

Summoning a waitress to the table, he said, "A rum punch, please . . . make that a double." He had the aggressive posture of a self-made man with an expense account.

"Thanks," Leslie said, now offering him a kindness: "Didn't I see you with that pretty little girl in the pink dress a few nights ago?"

"Yes, that was my daughter." He beamed. "I have her for Christmas." Along with the girl, Leslie figured, he had also brought golf clubs and a Fiberglas tennis racket to keep himself company. "It's a good time to be with her. Back home I find I'm so tied up all the time that I can't give Patty the attention I'd like."

"I assume you're divorced," Leslie mumbled.

"Yes."

The waitress set down the drink and a bowl of popcorn. Leslie grabbed a clump, all warm and salty in her hand. The others picked out one piece at a time. Berating herself for being such a glutton, she wondered why she could not have settled for an evening of entertainment at the casino instead of going for broke. What was this need inside herself? Self-indulgence? Self-flagellation? She gobbled up gambling chips like popcorn, which seemed irresistible at that moment but was guaranteed to make her sick later.

Leslie was glad, though, of this intermission, a chance to regroup before her mother zoomed in on her. Sarah Rittman could never leave well enough alone. Her detailed inquiries tended to have a cobweb effect; she worried and the children in turn worried, creating a maze of anxiety and excessive concern.

It was a brief intermission. Her mother appeared with a flush of curiosity, of the discomfiting kind, on her face. Her eyes, like an X ray searching for a surreptitious malignancy, scanned the room and instantly picked up Leslie. Moving across the room, she practically fell over her own frantic walk. She made a short stop, resting her hand flat against Leslie's back for leverage and blurted out a greeting. "What's wrong that you're so cross. On edge?"

"I just hate hearing about plane reservations," Leslie muttered. "It means I have to go back to work."

Bernie, seconding the motion, pulled out a chair for her mother, who promptly rested her case and ordered a Pernod straight up. On the advice of her judge-husband about not getting owned by outsiders, she never accepted a free drink; she finger-wrestled with Bernie over the tab, and won.

Mrs. Rittman's attention was drawn to a woman approaching the table. Leslie recognized her mother's patio guest.

"Hi," Sarah said and effusively introduced her: "This is Assemblywoman Carla Baker of New York."

Dressed in a pink knit top and polyester pants that revealed more than ample hips, the woman immediately launched into a speech. "I was delayed," she apologized, "on a call from my office about a subcommittee I'm chairing on battered women."

"Physical or psychological?" Leslie asked fliply. "Wives, daughters, employees, or all of the above?"

"We're looking at the entire problem," she replied with granite seriousness. "No area is sacrosanct."

Leslie smarted. "I would hope not."

"Our investigation," Assemblywoman Baker said imperiously, "will take in every segment."

"Very good." Leslie exchanged a smirk with Joanna.

The assemblywoman's looks, the mousy brown hair framing a plain, not unattractive horsy face, appeared to cover all bases, too. Carla Baker, she thought, could easily pass for an Ivy League WASP, the quintessential suburban housewife or just your neighborhood feminist.

The judge rushed into the bar. Searching for Sarah, his

gaze was more impatience than a compliment. "Dear," he commanded, "let's have dinner." He gave Bernie, who held out his hand, a cursory nod and smiled briefly at Joanna.

"Bye," Leslie said to them.

"Where's Rebecca?" he asked his wife, as if calling a witness to the stand.

"She's on some person's yacht."

"Why does she have to run around like that? Come on, the table's waiting."

In the dining room, Sarah quickly claimed the seat that belonged to Rebecca, next to her husband. She seemed gleeful as a child just given a new toy, but too shy to acknowledge it. "Here"—she orchestrated the seating—"you sit across from me, Carla, and next to my husband."

Jason and Holly dribbled over to the table. They looked as if they recognized the assemblywoman but could not place her in this setting.

Sarah introduced them. "Hi," they both said, then tuned out.

"Jason, *who* was that man in the bar?" Sarah asked in an accusatory voice, grabbing at her son's attention.

"Mom," Jason said defensively, "he's Ringo's agent."

"Who?"

"Ringo Starr," Jason repeated in an exasperated tone. "One of the Beatles."

"Oh."

It amazed Leslie that her mother read four newspapers a day and did not know who Ringo was. On the other hand she seemed to devote as much attention to shutting out information as absorbing it. She operated from a definite point of view and accumulated details to support it. Leslie knew the motivation was more fear than small-mindedness.

The assemblywoman, a more comfortable presence than a musical genius's agent, addressed Leslie's mother. "I hope we'll see more of you in the legislative chambers. I had the pleasure of attending a conference where you spoke."

"Where?" Sarah perked up.

"At the Hilton . . . on unwed mothers."

"I thought that topic went out with the fifties," Leslie snorted.

The assemblywoman glared at her, and she returned the look. "We just can't begin to cope with the incidences of venereal disease in the high schools," Carla Baker persisted. "The whole area of teenage sexuality is a matter of enormous concern."

What, Leslie wondered, could this woman possibly know about sexuality, teenage or otherwise. Assemblyperson Baker, as she probably liked to be addressed, had all the lyricism and sensuality of Betty Crocker. She was so tight-assed that she even wore stockings in the tropics.

Ms. Baker could not be sidetracked. "The statistics show a sixty-three percent increase. We simply don't have the funding to even begin to tackle the magnitude of this problem."

Jason butted in. "I'm hungry. Let's order. Anyone else for steak?"

A waiter stood over the table and counted all the hands, every one, for filet mignon, and returned momentarily with their salad.

"Would you like wine?" asked the judge.

"Let's get the Chateauneuf-du-Pape," Jason piped up.

"My son," Judge Rittman told the assemblywoman, "has lavish tastes. He's very accomplished at signing tabs in his father's name."

Jason smoldered. His ears turned a deep shade of red, almost frostbite purple. Shaking with anger, he kept tapping the bridge of his eyeglasses. Why did they keep coming back for more punishment?

Leslie patted Jason's back and grieved for him. He had followed his father's program exactly and failed to grasp the price of such compliance. He continually sought approval. Had Jason defied his father, he might have better understood the rejection. Warning Jason that by the time he got his Ph.D., all the judge's contacts would be too old to train him, Theodore Rittman assured him that he would not get any job offers elsewhere on account of a depressed economy. Now, with a lucrative Wall Street position and a promotion in under six months, Jason was labeled by his father a "prig" and a "schoolboy who thinks he's a big married man."

Drifting back in time to distance herself from the attack on her brother, Leslie wondered what had happened over these twenty-five years, since that morning she and Rebecca had sat with the nurse in the faded brown den waiting for their parents. Around noon, Daddy, his navy overcoat sprinkled with snowflakes, walked through the door. In his arm he held a life-size doll with curly brown locks, shiny almond eyes and lashes thick as feathers. "You have a brother," he beamed. "Mommy is fine. She has to stay in the hospital a few days to keep him company. He's a beautiful little boy. His name is Jason. He looks just like this doll."

While their father repaired to his room to dash off notes—"at last, a son!"—the girls practiced on the doll how they would behave with their baby brother. Propping the Jason doll on the piano stool, Leslie moved his plastic hands across the keyboard. Alternately, she told him, "You have to learn chopsticks," and "We love you a lot, Jason." Rebecca, her porcupine-quill hair shooting off in a dozen directions, kept falling down from the force of her own screaming and sobbing. Her white baby shoes, caked with polish not fully dry, left marks on the floor.

By evening the Jason doll's arms had been pulled out of

their sockets from all the squeezing, pushing and hugging to get its attention. The sisters sat on the chilly wooden floor, cushioning themselves with stuffing that had popped out of the doll. In the corner of the room the Jason doll lay hurt, but with a glint still in its eyes.

Surveying the demolition work, their father asked sorrowfully, "What happened?"

They began to sob.

Lifting both daughters in his arms he carried them upstairs to bed and tucked them in. "The damage is already done," he said woefully. "I'll get you a new doll tomorrow. You will be very happy to have a brother. He'll be coming home in a few days. He's prettier than the doll. He loves you both."

She was awakened from her reverie by Carla insisting in her politician's voice, "The governor's budget may have some unpleasant shocks, in terms of social-services cutbacks."

Were it not for the judge's disdain for yawning, he might have done so at this moment. "This is the Fall of the Roman Empire all over again," he sighed. "The whole society is coming apart. Saving one individual won't make any difference."

Leslie half-agreed with him, but expressed it differently, lashing out, "It's all bullshit. . . ."

Her father halted the ranting. Pointing a finger at her, he bellowed, "Leslie, why are you so resentful?"

"*What!*" she shrieked in disbelief. "Damn it, I'm a reporter. I see all the waste, these studies and reports with the fancy bindings."

"You're resentful," he taunted. "Carla deserves respect."

"What has this got to do with her?"

"You're attacking her."

"No, I'm not."

Leslie lied. She despised this woman, not only for her single-minded lack of imagination, but also for the way she claimed Sarah's attention. She could never remember having a conversation with her mother about anything that mattered to her. Usually they sat in the same room and smoked cigarettes together to pass the time. Now her mother was talking animatedly with a complete stranger about unwed mothers and teenage sexuality when Leslie had had to learn about her period on a blackboard in a friend's playroom. With a piece of white chalk, Ginny Katz's older sister had made diagrams of the ovaries, which she copied out of a high-school biology book, and then traced with a ruler what would happen at puberty. When the day of reckoning had arrived, Leslie had come home to a kitchen table laden with freshly baked cream puffs. Doubled over from cramps, she had worried that the pastry might cause her to bleed to death and had gone directly to bed to recover from this accident of nature.

She heard her father, attempting to smooth over the tension, inquire of Carla, "Are you going to remain in the Assembly another term?"

"As a matter of fact," she said, "I'm thinking of throwing my hat into the ring for mayor."

"Let us know," Sarah encouraged, "so we can make a contribution."

"Sure," the judge said, "we'd be happy to do that for you. And the children can pitch in, too."

Damn, Leslie bristled, if she would even give this boor a vote! Fuming at the idea of Carla Baker's campaign coffers being a thousand richer, she realized the subject of money was too touchy right now and kept quiet. A gambling debt just wouldn't stack up with a political shot.

The hotel manager, decked out in red Bermuda shorts and a green jacket to celebrate the holiday season, walked toward them. "Good to see you all back," Guy squealed, circling the table to give each one of them a peck on the cheek, but stopping—like a gnat in front of a lion—before their father. "I've been off the island and only got back an hour ago."

"Has it been busy here?" Sarah asked. Hungering for conversation that kept her at a comfortable distance from people and did not interrupt her loneliness for too long, she saved the rest of her questions about the food, shortage of towels and ratio of Jews to Christians for future chats.

"We have a full house right now," he said. "I'm glad I could get away before the season really takes off. We're booked straight through May."

"It's important to get away," Sarah agreed. "I go to Sardinia the whole of August."

The waiter reappeared with a tray stacked with pastries, giving Guy time to pull out a silver comb and smooth a blond hair curling like a spring on his forehead. Leslie breathed a sigh of relief that he did his beauty preparation on the other side of the table. She had a peculiar aversion to hair, even a silky lock blending with a napoleon, in her food. Now Guy rested his hands on the back of her sister-in-law's chair and inspected the large jade ring on his finger.

"Please have some dessert," the judge offered.

"No thanks," he said, patting his flat stomach. "I never indulge."

"Oh, Guy," Sarah said with urgency, "while you're here I'd like you to know that there was no hot water for a good part of the afternoon."

"It's a terrible problem," he sighed. "We've had very little rain on the island all year."

"It just poured the other day when my husband arrived," Sarah rejoined. "I was so worried. He never gets away."

A diamond-clad older woman waved him over. "Well, I'm glad I got to see all the Rittmans before you left," Guy said, making his own getaway.

A couple at the next table got up. The wife's lavender dress, billowing in the soft wind, brushed against Leslie's arm. Tickled by the cotton cloth, she turned around and looked up at azure eyes and a generous mouth.

The woman paused and said with obvious delight, "You're a wonderful tennis player. We caught the end of your match."

"Thanks."

As she spoke, her husband, his gray hair like a freshly minted coin, squeezed her tiny waist, an attractive inset in a firm, ample body. A woman of great élan, Leslie observed, someone who could sashay through a Cole Porter song.

Looking up at her and then down at the table, Leslie's father said, "Why don't you join us?"

Directly, without boring everyone with an apology about a possible intrusion, she took up the invitation. "I'm Erica Stone." She smiled warmly. "My husband, Jonathan."

Stone. Jew? WASP? A hybrid Jew. Bennington or Sarah Lawrence, or perhaps she had not bothered to attend in the first place. Park Avenue, but no Hamp, Hamp, Hamptons in the summer. Probably Florence, to visit the museums and vineyards. Standing somewhere between debutante Papagallo pumps and West Side Jewish intellectual sandals. Freckles blending into a golden tan. Forty, youthful, not girlish. Silky blond hair clothing a swanlike neck. An urban wood nymph, this Erica Stone, ethereal, eluding definition.

The judge and Erica's husband pulled out the same chair for her and stared at it and each other. She edged into it gracefully. "What would you *both* like to drink?" offered the judge, catching a quick frame of Erica in the corner of his eye.

"Whatever you are all having," the husband said in an easygoing, affable way.

"No, please," the judge insisted, "order what you like."

"Then I'll have a Seven-Up," Erica said. "We've got to

get an early start tomorrow."

"You're leaving . . . where?" the judge sputtered. He seemed shocked by his own reaction, the dejection in his voice.

"We'll be sailing around the islands for a month."

Launching into her favorite resort quiz game, Sarah asked, "How long have you been coming to the island?"

"This is our first visit," Erica replied. "We like to try new places every holiday."

When Christmas arrived each year Leslie also thought of going elsewhere, on a sailing expedition, African safari, Nepal, riding the Colorado Rapids, skiing in St. Moritz, crocodile-hunting in Colombia. But so convinced was she that her survival depended on staying close to the clan that she ended up cowering on a chaise longue in a family war zone on a Caribbean beach.

"This is our fifteenth Christmas in a row," her mother boasted. "Then I try to get down here as many long weekends as possible."

Smirking, Jason stole her next line: "But the people have changed. It's just a different group now."

Leslie filled in the next. "A lot of guests left because the food was going downhill. But I understand they have a marvelous chef this year."

Sarah toasted her good fortune with a sip of wine. "With what my husband spends on these trips," she remarked, "we could have bought three houses here by now."

"Dear," Judge Rittman said sternly, "let's not have a discussion." His tone clearly expressed his irritation. While other men had their Miami Beach-Beverly Hills talks about tans and tennis, he considered such conversations a waste of his precious work time.

Sarah's lips quivered, and her cigarette fell from her mouth. "You've had enough to drink"—her husband pounced—"and get rid of that cigarette." Leslie shuddered at her mother's obedience, sensing that the chatter about money and houses was a consolation prize; that she had struck a bargain, pathetic as it was, along the way. But what a price—the talk in her husband's presence was marked down from Sarah's otherwise intelligent discourse.

A silence like a sledgehammer fell on the table. Carla seized it to introduce herself. "I'm Assemblywoman Baker of New York. Pleased to meet both of you."

The Stones nodded at her. "I think," Jonathan advised his wife, "we should turn in pretty soon."

The judge held Erica for a moment in an admiring glance. "It's still early," he argued. "What's your hurry?"

"We have packing to do," Erica replied, "and we want to be fresh in the morning. Good-night, everyone."

"They seem like lovely people," Sarah remarked, glossing over her husband's flicker of flirtation with another woman. She was so totally selfless, even to the point of allowing him this moment of invigoration. Or was the freedom she allotted her husband a kind of insurance that he would not violate it? Still, there was not a petty bone in her body; she had an innocence at times so touching as to be almost comical. Leslie remembered tenderly how her mother scouted nuthouses, as though they were country clubs or summer camps, the summer Leslie thought herself homicidal after catching a boyfriend in bed with someone else in her apartment. The shrink had advised against hospitalization, diagnosing the problem as a severe case of betrayal. Though it would have broken her mother's heart to see one of the children committed, she made some inquiries at Leslie's insistence. "You wouldn't be happy stuck in the city all summer," she said. "Payne Whitney has a facility in the country with tennis courts and a swimming pool." Leslie went off to Europe to recover instead.

Rebecca breezed into the dining room. Her hair, all salty and disheveled, was bunched on top of her head. She looked gorgeous, windswept and golden-tanned, in a white wrap. She sat down in her mother's usual seat at the opposite end of the table from her father.

"Sooooo?" Rebecca joked in a Yiddish accent, to ward off an interrogation from her father.

Caught off guard, but evidently tickled by the ploy, he grinned and pretended to issue a command. "Come over here and give me a kiss."

"Daddy!"

He relented. "Did you have dinner?"

"Yes."

"Are you sure?"

"What?" Rebecca shot back impatiently. "I can't hear you from here."

"Now you know how it feels to sit there," Sarah huffed. "You can't hear anything your father says."

Rebecca and the judge both looked stunned. He reached for his wife's hand and patted it to soothe the damage from all those years she had been exiled to the far end of the table.

The scraping of chairs as guests turned to face the stage signaled the start of the show and distracted everyone at the table from this awkward moment. A pianist trilled a few notes of what sounded like a forties tune.

"What's that?" asked Rebecca, scowling.

"A friend of mine is singing," Leslie said defensively. "She's supposed to be very good."

"How come I never heard of her then?"

Leslie glared at her. "You don't even know her name."

"What is it? Myrtle McGuire?"

"Cut it out," Leslie snapped. "Her name's Joanna Rowe. And she's going on the Sally Henry Show when her album comes out."

The judge sneered. "Come on, Leslie," he said. "Why would she be performing at a Caribbean hotel if she were any good? She'll sell two copies of the album—both to you."

"If you know her so well," Rebecca persisted, "then what's her sign?"

Jason joined in the game. "Which house is rising in her chart?"

Their father leaned forward and, placing his hands squarely on the table, grunted, *"House?* How could anyone who grew up in *our* house believe in such nonsense?"

The assemblywoman got up to leave. "She's probably a Republican," she cracked. "In any event I don't think I want to force myself to stay awake to listen. Thank you all for a lovely evening."

"And Good Night!" Leslie said under her breath, red outrage gripping her neck and vibrating the muscles. "Carla, and Teddy and Ethel and Bobby . . ."

Her mother winced. "I hope we'll see you tomorrow," she called out to the politician.

Joanna came on stage in a purple caftan that gave her complexion a healthy blush. A spotlight jumped all over her before landing firmly in one spot. The audience was quickly captivated by her voice as she belted out a Cole Porter tune, even disarming the judge, who moved his hands like a conductor reaching for *sotto voce* to quiet everyone at the table. Swooning, his face in his hands, he looked as if he had a toothache. "She's tremendous," he groaned. "Absolutely first-rate." Inside this appreciation, some incarnation of his constant criticizing, Leslie recognized her father's demand, as unremitting as ever, for excellence.

"Leslie," he said as Joanna took a bow, "ask her if she'd like to have an after-dinner drink."

She gave Rebecca an indignant look and, feeling vindicated, walked to the stage to fetch the singer.

"You're great," the judge said. "Will you join us for a drink? Would you like something to eat too?"

"Thank you very much," she responded, "but I think I'm going to head straight for bed."

"Just sit for a minute and have something," he insisted. "We'll get you something fast."

"Okay, but only a minute, because I think I may collapse. I'm a great fan of your daughter Leslie. I read all her articles."

"Yes," the judge said, "she's a fine reporter."

A waiter stood over the table with a bottle of champagne crooked in his arm. "Dis is for you, ma'am," he told Joanna. "Dom Perignon 1973, dah finest." He set the bottle in a cooler and then removed a tiny white envelope from his jacket pocket.

Joanna sliced open the envelope and held the card close to a candle to study it. "Eddie," she said quizzically. "Who is Eddie Harmon?"

"He's the man from the casino, I think," Jason said.

"Go and find him," the judge instructed. "Tell him to join us for a drink."

Leslie's stomach clenched as she bent her head, sticking her nose into her champagne glass in order to peer over the rim at him without attracting his or anyone else's attention. Eddie stood with his back against the bar, scratching the biceps of his powerful freckled arms. A grin slit his face. Leslie tried to sip the champagne, but her throat was too dry to accept it. Eddie gulped down his drink in one shot, slid the glass at the bartender and followed Jason to the table.

"Hi," he said.

"Please sit down," the judge said.

"No, thanks," Eddie said. "I've got to be getting back to work soon. I just wanted the lady to know how much I admired her singing."

"Thanks," Joanna said curtly. "Do you know everyone here?"

"I think I've had the pleasure of seeing some of these faces in my place," he said, glancing around the table to lay claim to this familiarity and fixing his gaze a moment longer on Leslie.

She tightened her grip on the long-stemmed glass wobbling in her hand. The champagne splattered the table. Bubbles glistening on her tan skin, she wrung out her hands to disguise their trembling.

Eddie fidgeted and cracked his knuckles. "Your show was terrific," he said. "I haven't heard entertainment like that on this island in a century."

"Thanks," Joanna said, looking distantly at him, her coldness seeming almost familiar.

"Okay," he said disconsolately, "I have to be going. Nice to see you all. Bye." He looked directly at Leslie before he turned to go.

His loafers clicked on the floor. Leslie watched with relief as he walked off, rubbing the nape of his neck in an agitated motion.

The waiter, who was hovering over the table, chuckled. "Only dah fools go dere to dah casino."

Handing him a ten-dollar tip, Leslie's father said, "You're quite right. Thanks."

Leslie excused herself to go to the bathroom. The champagne left her with a floating sensation. Buoyed by Joanna's slight of Casino Eddie, the subtle slap in the face she herself had wanted to give him, she felt inured at this moment to the mess she was in.

As she turned the corner past the front desk, Eddie stood in her path, bending over the tennis chart posted there.

"Did you talk to your father?" he muttered angrily.

"Wh-what?" she stammered. She was immobile.

He squeezed her elbow and gave her a little shove. "You heard me," he hissed. "Don't get smart with me."

"Tomorrow," she said. "I promise."

"You've got exactly twenty-four hours," he snapped.

The menacing look on his face changed instantly into a half-smile at an approaching guest. Eddie turned and strode off.

Leslie opened the women's room door, practically falling against it. She felt heady from the perfumes in what seemed a motionless bowl of air. With the windows shut, the place felt like a steam bath. The mirror was fogged up. She plopped down on a toilet seat to try to get her balance and stop the dizzying turn of the room. The pinkish outlines of a newly-forming bruise started to blotch her elbow. Eddie had put the squeeze on her, literally.

She headed back to the table, but saw that the family had moved onto the terrace, where they were sipping brandy. Joanna was gone. But she could feel Eddie's sullen presence a few tables away, clinking the ice in his drink and then setting down the glass forcefully. With a money clip overflowing with hundred-dollar bills he signaled a waitress. He rose from the table and kicked his chair into place, a move that drew exasperated looks from the steel band players.

Rebecca yawned. "I'm falling off my feet from the boat. I've got to sleep."

Leslie jumped up from the table to make sure she had company on the way back to the room. "Mom," she asked, "do you have a sleeping pill?"

Her father demanded, "What do you need that for?"

"I haven't been able to sleep well because of the tree frogs," she stammered. "I just want to get a whole night's rest."

Sarah opened her pocketbook and took a pill out of a plastic bottle. If only, Leslie wished wearily, there was a casino potion in this portable pharmacy to make her problem vanish.

Inside the room she wondered about putting herself out

like this. She swallowed the pill and waited. It did not seem to be working. She felt like someone who, having stayed up around the clock, moved about in a rapid, yet slurred, state. She struggled with sleep, wanting to fall into it before Rebecca put out the light. The concentration she devoted to this self-imposed deadline kept her awake. Then, suddenly, she began to drift, moving into sleep, as she groped within her mind for an anchor to hold her to the bed. She let go at a moment when no one, including herself, could pull her out of it. . . .

A scream came from the next cottage, catapulting Leslie out of bed. She rushed into her brother's room. Holly was sitting up in bed, terrified. She swore she had heard whispering and someone trying to break in. A flashlight shone in Leslie's eyes. Squinting, she was able to make out the outline of what appeared to be a huge, knotty man. She moved back, but was caught inside the circles of his flashlight.

"Hold on, mahn," a voice said, the shadow of the body disappearing from view as he moved in on her.

"Ye-es." She shuddered. "Who are you?"

"Security, mahn."

He looked like an overstuffed kid, with spooky dark sunglasses framing a baby face. His hair was a kinky crewcut. "I'm Samson deh Strong Mahn of dah West Indies," he said, flashing an ID bracelet to back up his claim.

"Okay," Jason said, "come in."

"Don't you worry," he said. "We be sure to take good care of dah fahmily."

Holly whined, "I'm scared."

"Whoever it was has gone," Samson said. "And we find no footprints in dah sand."

"Jason," Holly persisted, "what are we going to do?"

"Not much," he said sleepily, "except go back to bed and get a night's sleep."

"You're not being respectful of my feelings," she complained. "If I say someone was outside and I'm scared, you shouldn't just toss it off lightly." No matter the circumstance, Holly would inject roadside psychiatry into it. If someone held a machete up to her neck, she would no doubt want to have a discussion about allowing people to breathe.

"Damn it, Holly," he shouted, "grow up and stop being so scared all the time."

At the outset of the marriage, Jason had been drawn in by Holly's fears, somehow enjoying her frailty because of the strength he gained from the protective role. Now he was disgusted. His sisters had certain fears, but their sum total could not match those of Holly, who panicked at a wave or a tennis ball coming at her.

Samson, sounding more like a marriage counselor than security chief, agreed to have another look around, though he said he did not expect to find much. He poked around some hibiscus bushes and baby palms encased in pineapplelike cones around the cottage. Five minutes later he reappeared to present his findings. "Dere is no trace whatsoever of anyting or any person."

The curtains moved slightly, enough to bunch up against the open window.

"Could you check behind them?" Holly asked tentatively.

"No probelem." He separated them slowly. Jumping back on both feet, as if playing hopscotch, he bent over to look again. Leslie felt numb. Samson pulled the curtains apart. A giant lizard jumped out, evoking another scream from Holly and one from Samson as well.

Fed up with this mockery of her predicament, Leslie stuck her hand between the jalousies and reached for the lizard, but it eluded her grasp. She tried again, this time pulling hard on its tail. The tail fell off and slithered to the floor, and the lizard's body lay dead on the screen. Picking up both parts, Leslie stepped outside and deposited them on the beach, then kicked sand over the mutilated lizard for a proper burial.

Much as Leslie wanted to throttle her sister-in-law, she could not shove aside a belief that Eddie was about. This was no false alarm.

Samson escorted her back to her room. "Notting to worry yourself over," he reassured Leslie. "I be watch dah fahmily."

"Thanks."

Careful not to awaken Rebecca, she tiptoed into the bathroom. With the light off, she fumbled for her toothbrush and soap, turning the faucet a crack to avoid a gushing sound that might signal her return to the room. She went back to bed but sat up, on top of the blanket. She imagined a knock at the door, not from a smiling waiter bringing cocktails, but from one of Eddie's underlings poised to hurl acid in her face. Her eyes darted around the room. She desperately needed to sleep, to revive her strength in case she needed to do battle. She succumbed just as the morning light affronted her tired body.

13

A tentative knock, as though meant to be taken back, came at the door. There was a second knock, this one more confident, that lifted Leslie out of a daze somewhere between sleeping and waking.

"Just a minute," she called out.

Turning on her side, Rebecca grumbled, "You woke me," and went back to sleep.

An islander Leslie recognized with relief as belonging to the hotel staff bent back some plants as he stood in the dirt and talked through the screen.

"Who is Miss Leslie Rittmahn?"

"Me," she said in a self-accusatory tone. She could never remember being so ashamed to answer to her own name.

"Dere's a call for you."

"Coming," she said. Nervously, she slipped out of her nightgown and yanked on a swimsuit.

Outside, a silk screen of dark clouds floated over pastel sketches of daybreak, depriving her momentarily of the sun's warmth. She felt humiliated and naked running to take a call at this hour. Checking to make sure the hotel messenger was not studying her rump, she saw him sifting a plastic glass out of the sand a few feet away.

At the desk the phone was off the hook, lying on its side. She picked it up. "Hello," she stammered, twirling the cord in her fingers and binding her knuckles in its coils.

There was no sound. She shook the phone. Out came a holler that seemed to reverberate through the lobby. "You think you're too good for me, sitting there last night with your fancy family." Leslie tried to muffle his voice by practically screwing the receiver to her ear. "Your daddy doesn't know the half of it, about his daughter."

Eddie sounded totally irrational, as if he had been kept up all night by rage, going over and over in his mind a slight, real or imagined, scratching his psyche until it was raw, the fury growing with insomnia.

"I've moved up your deadline," he thundered. "It's five o'clock!" The voice dropped to a conversational pitch. He blew air through his teeth as if fanning the words. "I expect a call by five—not a minute after." Then, quietly, he hung up the phone.

Leslie wobbled into the bar, stepping over a mound of dirt swept into a neat pile to be carted off. A few dirty glasses, with residues of beer and diluted scotch the color of urine, were lined up on top of it. Off to the side there was a coffee pot, quarter-full, enough for two or three cups, but turned rancid and tar-black overnight. Much to her distaste, she switched on the Mr. Coffee for a shot of caffeine. Falling into a chair again, she massaged her eyes, pressing so hard that stars appeared on the black horizon of her lids. She heard the coffee gurgling and poured some in a cup with a rust-colored ring coating the bottom. With a plastic spoon she dumped in a hard lump of powdered cream. The sugar was damp and sticky with the wing of a dead fly on top of it. As she stirred the murky coffee, she felt spent, used up, stale.

"Do you know where I could get some cigarettes?" she called out to a man who was dunking the bar glasses into soapy water that smelled like grease.

He walked around front, unbuttoned a shirt pocket, pulled out a pack and handed her one. "Everyting close up till ten dis morning," he said.

She wrestled the cigarette into her mouth and took a long puff on it. "Thanks a lot. Could you spare a few extra?"

"No probelem." He obliged, setting the rest of the pack on the table with a box of matches. "I get more latah."

She pumped herself with coffee, refilling the cup, and cigarettes, lighting one off the next, almost choking herself. Her mind speeded up, thoughts whizzing by, colliding, and she could not hold on to a single firm plan of action. Too edgy to get control of herself, she fueled herself with uppers, which only dragged her down and spurred her to total destruction. She worried about how her body could take the abuse, its circulatory system a network of rusty pipes too clotted with nicotine and caffeine to flush out the booze from the previous night.

The breakfast staff were starting to arrive, their chatter and laughter, along with the clanking of plates and silverware, distracting her. The aroma of freshly baked bread and croissants wafted through the room.

"You be up real early tah-day," the headwaitress said, bending over the table. "I try to get you someting. Anyting for dah fahmily."

"Thanks," Leslie yawned. "Whatever you have."

Nothing revived her. The freshly squeezed orange juice gave her heartburn. Her mouth was dry and burning and her breath fetid. The croissant stuck to the roof of her mouth, almost making her gag. She smoked another cigarette and stared at the sea creased with waves, bigger than usual, that smacked against each other. A wind combed the palm trees, separating the fronds into porcupine spines, all silky and glistening from the sheen of sun trying to break through the clouds. A green papaya, not yet ripe, lodged inside a tree, looking bloated and distended like a pregnant belly. The island seemed distorted. A cloud bank was breaking, disintegrating into morning.

An elderly couple walked briskly into the dining room. They always showed up first on the beach, probably to get the most wear out of the day. Their rested, eager faces affronted Leslie, who cursed herself for the mess she was in. She decided to go to her room and get cleaned up.

Rebecca stood wrapped in a towel, about to jump into the shower, but when she saw Leslie she parked herself instead in a chair. To Leslie's surprise, she was not furious about being awakened earlier. "Who was calling you at that hour?" she probed.

"It was someone else they wanted," Leslie stammered.

"You sure were gone a long time."

"I figured as long as I was up I'd wait for breakfast."

Rebecca tried a more direct line of questioning. "Is anything wrong?"

"No," Leslie said. Exhaustion reduced her panic to an offhanded resignation.

"It just seems like something is bothering you. What's up?"

Leslie yawned to hold back the words. She desperately needed to talk to someone about her problem. Yet she felt that her sister's concern did not deserve the reward of a confession as burdensome as this.

"You can talk to me, Leslie," Rebecca said softly.

"There's nothing to say," Leslie replied solemnly.

"Okay," Rebecca said, reassuring, "but I'm here if you need me."

So distraught, Leslie could not locate a focus for her frustration and despair. Instead of making her sister a rain-catcher of tears, she set her up as a shooting target. "You haven't been here for me the whole trip," she sulked.

Rebecca looked hurt. "What do you mean?"

"You're always off somewhere," Leslie whined, "and you never think to include me."

"You never want to come along," her sister answered, "so I don't bother to suggest anything. I figured you would ask me. I'm sorry if I hurt you."

"You did."

Rebecca unleashed her own pains. "I've always looked up to you my whole life," she began.

"Don't!"

Oblivious to Leslie's command, Rebecca sputtered, "The way you always get everything done, approach people for all your stories, never give up."

"That's professional stuff," Leslie said glumly. "It's just a front."

"I know," Rebecca soothed. "I just wish you weren't so vulnerable."

"How so?" Leslie squinted.

"Look," Rebecca blurted out, "Daddy's very concerned about the way you seem—so withdrawn. He thinks you're unhappy."

"What is he talking about?"

"You heard what I said, Leslie," her sister insisted. "You refuse to accept it. You and Daddy are a pair. You won't listen, and he doesn't know how to talk to you. He feels that the wrong word could push you over."

"He has an impressive vocabulary," Leslie said sardonically. "Moron, idiot, wastrel, ad infinitum."

Rebecca started to speak, then paused to rethink what she would say next. "He loves you," she said simply. "He asked me to tell you this."

Leslie felt like crying, but knew if she started she would not be able to stop. "Thanks," she said weakly.

Rebecca respected her embarrassment at hearing this news and shifted the topic. "Do you want to shower first?"

"Thanks."

"For what?"

"Letting me go ahead of you."

Rebecca opened the bathroom door a crack and called out, "Next time if you want to go somewhere, say so. We're supposed to be grown-ups and express ourselves."

The warm water washed over the tension in Leslie's body. She thought how dangerously close her sister had come to the casino problem and was glad now she had not inflicted it on her. For once she was not wailing like a baby, incontinent at the mouth, dumping her shit on someone else's lap.

By the time she dried herself and put her bathing suit back on, she felt in need of another shower. Clammy tremors struck her body. Perhaps the sea might have a more restorative effect, help her to think clearly.

On the beach she saw the assemblywoman pulling what looked like a report out of a briefcase and showing it to her mother. Leslie rushed past them into the sea, plunging into a rapid crawl. Lifting her head, she caught a glimpse of her father watching and dunked her head in the water again. She swam fast, her arms lashing the sea. Her heartbeat was racing. She paused, treading water to steady herself, and was surprised to see she was not far from shore but a quarter-mile down the beach. Regaining strength, she paddled herself farther out and then floated on her back awhile. The waves bobbed under her. Unable to anchor her mind on a single thought, she began to get seasick. Suddenly she felt sand digging into her back and a wave breaking over her. She struggled to get up but lost her balance and fell down again. She rolled over on her stomach and began crawling the few feet to shore. She had made a little progress when she felt pressure on her hands, as though someone were stepping on them. She lifted her head to see what was holding them down. Her fingers looked like toes. Leslie shut her eyes, certain that she was losing her mind.

"Need some help?" a stern voice said. The toes slithered away, revealing a sand sculpture of her buried fingers. She stared, no sound coming out of her mouth, through an archway of two legs, like thick tree stumps. "Oh, I'll get Daddy. To the rescue, Judge, come quick."

Just as she thought to fling herself backward into the water, Eddie yanked her arms, dragging her out, as if recovering a drowned body. "Just keep quiet," he said, and pushed her inside a restaurant-hut.

No one came to the rescue. Her predicament went unnoticed in a jangle of high-pitched voices outside the Yellow Bird, a local hangout with nonstop calypso music that carried for miles up the beach. Natives munched on rice and papaya. Children in diapers decorated with chicken feathers perched on their parents' heads. Teenagers splashed around in the shallow water. The people danced, their arms glistening with sweat, and swished their derrieres at flabbergasted tourists sipping tropical drinks and munching lobster sandwiches. Eddie shoved her onto a black picnic bench. Across the table his friend, in a Hawaiian print shirt, grinned at her. "How ya doing, Leslie?"

She sulked. Her eyes were screwed to Vince's tattoo, a heart with a Cupid's arrow shot through it, an outcast's badge along the resort strip.

He cracked to Eddie, "She wasn't doing so bad at your place the other night, huh? Not exactly a cold fish, wouldn't you say?'' He picked a piece of tobacco off his lip. "There are too many coloreds on these islands. Where's a man to find satisfaction? I don't want to catch no diseases.''

Leslie crinkled her nose in disgust, thinking he should only be so lucky to have an island woman even bother to look his way.

"Don't get so uppity," Eddie snapped. "Have a drink? How about you, Vince?''

Vince twisted his neck to look at Eddie's watch, the face turned inside his wrist. "No time, pal, my plane's leaving in an hour, at noon. Maybe you can fly Leslie here over some time for a night. It gets lonely with no broads."

"Get out of here," said Eddie, snorting with laughter. "She's not going anywhere."

"Yeah," he said, rising from the table and winking at her, "you got a contract or something on her."

"See you, Vince. . . . Give a call when you land.''

"Okay, pal.''

Leslie was glad of Vince's departure. It was bad enough to be seen with Eddie again. She worried about who knew of her messy situation. Since phone service, except for long-distance, was virtually nonexistent on the island, talk was communal, outside the Yellow Bird, in town, at calypso joints and clubs. Last week's uproar, reported all over downtown Anlucia, was about the transistor radio and aviator glasses that a Frenchwoman bought for a Rastafarian beach bum. Gossip spread like brushfire, unabated and searing, often forcing locals to flee to save face or a relationship. The stinging sun exposed Leslie in broad daylight.

"Some character, that Vince," Eddie chuckled. "No genius, but a good guy."

Withholding comment, Leslie stared coldly over his shoulder.

Eddie squinted his burnished face at her. "What's the matter you're so quiet? You better get on the stick and talk to Daddy."

"I'm going to speak with him today," she assured him. "And you'll have your money."

He glared at her across the table, leaned forward and gripped her chin. "I told you the money is no good," he fumed. "The case—I want it thrown out." It was as if sparks from his cold blue eyes pierced her like an ice pick. "Get it!" he hissed. "I said the *case*. Then I'll be off the hook. And I can walk. Free at last! The boss will owe me for saving his ass. I haven't even told him yet. I want it to be a big surprise. You think I like being an indentured servant on this lousy island? I'm surprised you're still sitting around some company when your old man's money could spring you in a second."

Money, yes. The money, Leslie thought. He *would* leave her alone if she got him the money. His lips had moved, but the words were lost in her panic. She would go to her father and ask him for ten grand and then turn the money over to Eddie. Back in New York she could wangle the cash in a week's time to repay him. The idea became a glimmer of hope, as if an unseen derrick had lifted a weight from her shoulders. She felt heady at the thought.

She perked up. "I'm going to find my father now and settle this."

"You better get back to me by five," he warned. "No later!"

"Sure." Heading back to the hotel beach, she spotted her father up ahead. She was relieved to see that he was alone. A towel covered his sunburned legs as he sat in a chair and underlined legal papers. She studied him from afar and imagined his face clouding with disappointment if she were to tell him what she'd done. How strange it was, she thought, that the concern her parents showed her as a child seemed to be turned inside out as they got up in years, with Leslie panicking at an urgent call from them. She felt close to tears whenever she had to say good-bye at an airport, wondering if this might be the last time.

She quickened her pace, figuring she would tackle him with her words. A conversation with the judge was like a contact sport. Hit him up fast from behind, she strategized, before he could parry with her. She slid to a stop in the sand before him, lost her breath, and with it her confidence. "Where's everyone?" she said weakly.

"They all went into town for some last-minute shopping," he replied. "Your mother was looking for you. She thought you would want to go along. You just missed them."

"Dad," she said shyly, "could I talk with you? Let's go for a walk."

He got up and folded the towel on the back of his chair. "Which way shall we go?"

She pointed in the direction opposite to the Yellow Bird. "Around the cove," she said. "Come to think of it, I haven't been over there to get my seashells this year."

Already he was four steps ahead of her, opening the discussion. "What's troubling you?"

"My job."

"Why should that be a problem?"

"I'm not being paid enough," she said glumly. "And I've been putting in nights and weekends. I work as hard as any lawyer."

"You have no financial pressures," he lectured. "Why should you be concerned?"

"No financial pressures," she shot back. "You must have been talking to my boss, who reads about the wealthy Rittman family in the papers and figures because I'm not divorced with two kids I don't need the money or the job in the first place."

"Is that my fault? You've all had plenty of advantages. How many reporters take Christmas vacations on Anlucia?"

"The sane ones don't," she hummed sardonically. "That's for sure."

"Leslie," he instructed, "you have it far better than the average American."

"Yeah . . . and my title isn't good enough either."

"Don't tell me," he chided, "you're worried about a title at that magazine. In the course of your lifetime what difference could it possibly make?"

"It's a matter of my dignity."

A woman with the proportions of a wrestler, complete with a thick neck and a long, open robe, made a flying leap over a sand castle. "What a fatnick," the judge said.

Seeing someone else that unattractive pumped confidence into Leslie. "My God, I don't believe she has the nerve to wear a bikini."

"Even more incredible," her father said, "is that such a body exists to fight its way into that suit. Leslie, don't trouble yourself with nonsense. If that's your only goal, then I'm disappointed in you."

"What I'd really like to do is write a book." She stared at her feet sweeping the sand around in a semicircular motion.

"Who's stopping you?" he said grudgingly.

"It's too piecemeal with the job," she said. "I want to quit."

"Is that wise?" he asked. "You know you'll be frantic without it. You're like me—you can't tolerate being idle."

"I wouldn't call writing a book being exactly idle," she grumbled. "And you said I never have to worry about money. That I have all the economic freedom in the world."

"What'll it take?"

"Ten thousand to live for a year."

"How do I know you'd do it?" he accused. "Five hours a day, seven days a week, without fail."

"I asked you for the money," she said, seething, "not a lecture. You know how hard I've worked my whole life."

"This is different," he parried. "I'm not going to finance an experiment. Remember that summer I sent you to Madrid and when I showed up couldn't find you because you were at a party?"

"I was eighteen," she wailed. "It was my professor's party after our last exam."

"I waited at the dormitory until after midnight," he said, "and I didn't hear from you until the next morning at my hotel."

"Talk about experiments," Leslie fumed. "What about that Carla Baker character? You're ready to give her a thousand. There's no guarantee with campaigns. It's like gambling, throwing your money in the wastebasket."

"It's important," he said. "And she's not in your position. She probably doesn't have any family behind her."

"Oh, politics," Leslie said. "I get it. Politics is God. All that matters. Well, I have some news for you. . . ."

He started to walk away, but she called him back with a taunt. "You talk like you're so generous," she screamed. "when you're only into petty control."

"How dare you speak to me like this!" His jaw flexed.

She raised her eyebrows skeptically. "Just forget I asked," she called out, understanding now that her problem went way beyond money. Just as he kept control, she had lost it in the casino by trying to get it back. She kicked over the sand castle and set about to build her own design for living, first by digging her way out of this mess. "Child's play," she sniffed, watching the moat cave in.

14

It was just her luck that at seven minutes to five a pear-shaped older guest, fingering a pink message slip, tied up the hotel phone. "Damn it," Leslie muttered impertinently, "I don't believe this." Each time it sounded as if he might be getting off he resumed the conversation. She tapped him and asked whether he would be much longer. Holding up a finger to indicate another second, he then found something else to talk about. The hands of the clock winked at her deadline, three minutes away, to call Eddie. She moved in on the man, breathing down his neck and grunting, "Shit . . . why doesn't he get off the damn phone." She paced up and down, tugged wildly at her hair and made more annoying noises, which now drew a disgusted look from the front-desk operator.

"What's your hurry?" the man huffed as he hung up. "You know, you're a very rude young lady."

"Fine," Leslie sniffed and paid him no further attention

as she snatched the phone away and barked instructions at the recalcitrant operator. "Dial four four six nine three . . . and connect it to the conference room."

When she picked up the phone she realized her hand was trembling and worried that her voice might betray the fear and loathing she felt for Eddie. Her heart was pounding so hard that she was convinced she was having a coronary.

"Yeah," answered a voice she was sure belonged to Eddie. The distracted, short-of-breath tone reminded her of someone interrupted during sex, evoking a sickening memory of her evening with him.

She strained to be civil, in the hope that the use of his last name conferred a respect that might soften him. "Mr. Harmon, please."

"Who's calling for him?"

"Leslie Rittman."

"Hang on," the voice said and disappeared for a moment, then came back on the line suddenly. "So what did your old man say?"

"Nothing," she mumbled vaguely. Leslie felt faint.

"What does that mean?" he snapped.

"I don't know." Her hand was cramping, and she could not straighten out her fingers or bend them.

"Well then," he said in a whisper, so cool as to be on the edge of an explosion, "I guess I'm going to have to come over and talk to your daddy to find out for myself."

"If I were you," she said, "I wouldn't try to talk to my father. It's not subtle, discreet. You could blow the whole deal."

"What deal?" he grumbled, his curiosity yielding a bit more leeway.

"I'm working out the final details," she said. "It's not a good idea to say too much over the phone."

He relented, grudgingly. "How does it look?"

"Excellent," she blurted out, then counseled, "Timing is

everything. I'll have it all finalized by eleven tomorrow."

"Where?" he pressed.

"Wherever you like," she said agreeably. "I could meet you on the beach at the end of the cove." There she would have privacy and yet remain within shouting distance of bathers.

"Nah," he growled. "I'll bring a boat around, and you swim out past the cove."

"It's definite," Leslie assured. "I'll be there. For certain."

Eddie hung up without further word.

"You tru?" the operator asked in a disapproving manner.

"Yes," Leslie mumbled, and rubbed her hand absently to loosen up the tense muscle as she left the lobby.

Back in the cottage Rebecca was napping, but she opened one eye to see who was there and then turned on her back and stretched her arms as if doing calisthenics. It seemed as though she were getting up especially for Leslie. "You're coming with me to Roz's party?" she asked.

"I'm not sure," Leslie replied. "Is that the woman who wears all that makeup in the middle of the day? The one whose husband thinks she's so glamorous."

Rebecca grinned. "I think I'll ask her how come her false eyelashes don't melt in the heat," she said. "It's a pleasure to see you again, Roz. Thanks for having us. I was just curious about one thing . . . the lashes."

"What time is the party?"

"It started at five and will go on late," Rebecca replied. Then—her way of showing remorse about not including Leslie in previous evenings—she urged, "Come. It's our last night. It'll be fun."

"Okay."

Leslie, damp and chilled, climbed into the shower. The water bounced off her shoulders, spraying her hair with a few unwelcome drops. Washing it now would be too risky, without the fast-drying effect of the tropical sun. She wanted to surround herself every minute with people.

As they walked toward the lobby a hotel guard, his crisp white uniform saturated with cologne, blocked their way. Staring fiercely at Rebecca, he questioned her, "Wan to go to dah town to dance tonight?"

She smiled and said, "I have a party."

"You don't like deh black mahn," he accused, letting his hand wander toward his crotch. "Wouldn't you like to try one?"

"I don't go with strange men I meet walking on the beach," she snapped, pushing Leslie to whisk her away. "Come on, let's get out of here."

Leslie's confidence in the protection offered by the hotel took a dramatic nosedive. The whole island was starting to stink of corruption. The prime minister's face, she remembered, was engraved on the one-dollar chips at the casino.

Shinehead slouched in a chair, waiting to take them up the hill, which was too rocky to ascend on foot.

"Where's everyone?" Leslie asked.

"Mommy and Daddy are coming in a little while," Rebecca said. "He's waiting for a call. And the married couple want to have dinner alone, in a quiet little corner. At least we won't have to hear Jason tell the same Mel Brooks joke for the hundredth time. He's been driving me crazy with it."

Shinehead made three abortive attempts to climb the steep hill and then, gunning the engine as if preparing to storm the place, reached the top. Observing the crowd on the terrace he remarked, "Dey be hav a lot of people tonight."

With little else to do on the island, it was easy to draw a large group, the hundred or so people who milled around there. As they entered the house a man blew a conch shell in Leslie's ear. Musical notes were supposed to emerge from the makeshift instrument, but he only mastered a few toots, like a foghorn, sufficient to get him some laughs around the place. Clutching her arm, he said, "You're one of the Rittmans. You all resemble each other. What do *you* do?" She hated being snagged like this and tried to pull away. He refused to let go.

"I'm a writer."

"Oh, you should meet my wife here, Rose," he said. "She paints."

"Hi," Leslie said briefly, imagining the flowers-by-numbers she probably did in her suburban basement. "I just finished a piece on Bob Rauschenberg."

"Who?"

"He rejected Abstract Expressionism . . ."

The husband released his grip. "Oh," he said, "Rose doesn't do anything like that."

The white concrete house hung over the harbor. There was a swimming pool and expensive Italian marble floors laid like linoleum tiles, probably the work of Anlucia artisans. The cobalt-blue sky was turning into charcoal velvet with diamonds.

Leslie looked away and saw Rebecca standing next to her. "What is there to eat? Otherwise, I'm leaving."

Rebecca led her to a buffet table, with baked ham, roast beef, potato salad, red snapper, stuffed crab, potato chips and kosher salami flown in earlier that day.

"Zabar's to the rescue," trilled the hostess, at her side her requisite gnome of a husband grasping her waist. "The salami came in on the noon flight. Eastern was four hours late. I was so worried it wouldn't arrive."

"It's a lovely party," Rebecca said politely. "We've been out of New York just long enough to be ravenous for a few slices of Hebrew National."

"Glad you both could come," Roz beamed.

The wife of a dentist nabbed them and started clicking off

the names, ages and interests of her four sons. "Neither of you girls are married, are you? You have such an extraordinary family."

Leslie wondered if the woman's enthusiasm would hold up under the knowledge that there was a degenerate gambler among the Rittman clan. She struggled to be gracious: "Your sons are terrific water-skiers."

"My husband," she said proudly, "taught the boys when they were very little."

"Great," Leslie said politely.

Though this was about the level of conversation she could manage at the moment, Leslie searched the faces in the room for an alert one. She landed on Joanna and instantly picked her way through a thicket of people to reach her.

"Hi. Glad to see you again."

"Same here," Joanna replied.

Someone grabbed Leslie from behind and whisked her away. "Where have you been?" he asked with robust cheer. "How come we haven't played?"

It was Drew Nash, a fortyish retired Englishman who had made his fortune in porno flicks, bingo games and the slots. His craggy face looked used up, but the green eyes and long lashes softened it. He was extraordinarily fit from tennis.

"I should ask *you* that," Leslie parried.

"No, it was up to you," he insisted, "to come and find me."

Leslie shrugged her shoulders disdainfully. At the level of this conversation, she did not have to wonder why she ended up in the casino. She edged away from him on the pretense of getting a drink. He pulled her back in. "Look," she stammered, "I was in the middle of talking to that woman."

"Who?"

"Joanna Rowe, the singer."

He looked puzzled. "Why would you want to talk to *her*?"

"Why not?"

"She's bad news." His words were clipped.

"How can you say such a thing about someone you hardly know?"

"I know one thing," he snorted. "That woman is Eddie Harmon's shill. She comes to the casino, plays blackjack for a few hours and always wins to draw people into the game."

"She's a singer," Leslie pleaded, as if begging him to change the story. She looked through a blur of pain at her friend, now moving out of the crowd, vanishing, her absence beginning to confirm this news.

"I think," Drew gossiped, "she's trying to break with Eddie. There's no question she can sing."

Leslie trembled with disappointment and fear. "If she's so tight with him," she challenged, "how come Eddie isn't here, too?"

"Maybe"—he smirked—"she's trying to pick up on someone else who can help her."

Rebecca came up behind her and poked. "What's wrong?"

"You know my friend Joanna," said Leslie, "the singer. I just found out she's a shill at the casino."

"Why are you so surprised?"

"What do you mean?"

Rebecca studied her oddly. "Daddy thought she was a fake."

"That's not what he told me," Leslie said weakly. "He thought she was a great singer."

"That also. But one thing has nothing to do with the other."

"I never heard him say that," Leslie persisted.

"You were in the bathroom," Rebecca said gently. "He said not to mention it because it wasn't important, and he was glad you made a friend here. Besides, we're leaving. By the way, he's on the terrace and wants to talk to you."

"About what?" she grumbled, her thoughts weaving in and out of anger like a hostile drunk.

"I don't know," Rebecca said, "except that he looks upset. At least hear what he has to say."

"Okay." She shrugged. On her way to finding him, she kept slipping between her conscious and unconscious minds. The moment she felt reconciled to the idea that the mess was hers to resolve, a rage blew up again, toppling all reason. Back and forth her feelings went.

Emerging onto the terrace she heard Mr. Katz, holding her father and three other people at bay, hollering about Israel, anti-Semitism and Blacks. For them to walk away, Leslie figured, would be to turn their backs on Almighty Israel and Mr. Katz. Maybe the words needed to be spoken over and over again, but Leslie refused to suffer another one of these monologues at a cocktail party.

"Not another dime for the Black bastards," Katz thundered. "They thought they were going to get money from the Arabs. NAACP—their solicitations go straight into the garbage. Incredible, how one minority can turn on another minority after all we've done for them!"

Leslie could not help wondering whether Jerome Katz cut off his childrens' allowance if they did not toe the line. Disgusted, she started to leave, but was caught in her father's searching glance. As she walked over, she noticed her host's face brighten, probably at the chance to launch into a sequel to Israel, anti-Semitism and Blacks, with Leslie and her generation of "Assimilateds" the new punching bag.

She was right on target. "The Jewish Experience is lost

on people your age," Katz greeted her. "*You* didn't live through the Holocaust. *I* knew it was going on. That Roosevelt was unconscionable."

"*Shalom,*" Leslie interrupted, lifting her wine glass in prayer. "*Boruch Atoh Adonoi, Elohenu, Melech Haolom, Borai Pri Hagofen.* I learned that at Shorty's Hebrew and Watersports Institute on Anlucia. Only they kept saying 'ha-dolphin' instead of 'ha-gofen.' The *shvartzers* never learn."

"If you'll excuse me," her father said, pulling Leslie aside, "I want to talk privately with my daughter."

"Good to see you both," Katz said. "Glad you could come."

Backing away, Leslie waved slyly at him, calling out, "*Shalom, shalom,* Mr. Katz."

She dreaded another confrontation with her father, coming at the worst possible time, on the heels of Israel—also his rod of negativism. If the judge had a migraine, found a hair in his soup or was angry at his law clerk, inevitably he introduced anti-Semitism into evidence at some point during the dinner-table conversation. At least, Leslie thought proudly, he did not blame the Blacks. But how many times, she raged, had she been subjected to his Katzian arrogance, admittedly more intelligent and literate, but producing the same effect on her, no ifs, ands or buts, just the Talmud According to Theodore Rittman. To contradict him was to have the wrath of God visited upon her. Thou Shalt Beat Thy Children's Minds into Plowshares and suffocate their imagination with the noxious fumes of hypocrisy. "*Never again,*" she screamed inside her mind.

Leslie was unaware of her father trying to draw her back, patting her wild head of curly hair and kissing her forehead. "I've decided to give you the money," he said. "It's not worth it for me to see you so unhappy."

Her anger was defused. She suddenly felt terrible about

lying to him and could not even consider accepting the money. "No," she said glumly, "you don't owe me anything."

"It's yours," he said softly. "I told you I'd let you write a book."

The anger swelled again, like a boil that needed to be lanced. "Isn't it enough that you won the Six-Day War?" she seethed. "You did it. It was your money. The Israelis might as well have been on holiday on Anlucia with soldiers of fortune like you and Katz to fight their battles. And while you're at it, why don't you both invest in annihilating Blacks?"

Astonished, he shook his head disconsolately. "Leslie," he said quietly, "you know I don't feel that way about Blacks. Have you ever heard me express or encourage intolerance or bigotry? The one thing I have tried to give my children is a sense of values and a love of learning and books, Jewish scholarship. I've tried my best. You must remember I'm a prisoner of my own background, too."

She looked at his proud Jewish face, the high intelligent brow rising to integrity, the strong mouth telling her to return the wallet she found outside the schoolyard, forbidding her to wear lipstick and stockings even though everybody else in her fifth-grade class was doing it and instructing that in the end there was no eluding the self. Now she remembered, guiltily, those school-year summers in Mexico and Madrid, even if he dragged her afterwards to Fonda del Sol to test her Spanish on some waiter who, having lived in New York forty years, knew only "Gracias." No one had invented a language for parents and children to talk to each other. She had been so busy pouting about his control, Leslie realized, she hardly ever thanked him for these opportunities. How ironic it now seemed that over the fifteen years of family holidays he had probably spent, on her alone, three times the casino debt. Yet the money had not saved her. Now, with his offer, she felt empty-handed, with no one to blame for her mess. She panicked a second about rejecting the money, but still could not bring herself to grab it. Leslie was ready, finally, to fight her own battles.

"The money is here for you." Her father sighed. He searched the terrace for the rest of the family. "I think we all better go now," he said, "if we want to get in the morning at the beach. We have to be up early to pack and leave. Could you find Rebecca, please?"

"Sure," she said, "we'll meet you at the car."

Moments later, with everyone in tow, Rebecca tapped on the window to wake Shinehead, who jumped up and stretched his arm sleepily over the front seat to unlock the door for them. Once they got in, he started up the car, then threw it into second gear and rode the brakes down the steep incline. Leslie was suddenly glad of the family's presence and felt safe in it. Even in her own apartment, she thought, it was never as comfortable as sleeping at home. She tricked herself, always, into believing the quiet of the country was the reason. Yet the island was more still, and Leslie had been unable to protect herself from her own self, now cowering from the adult life that was sneaking up on her like some nasty New York mugger.

15

"Leslie," her mother called through the window screen, "come out before the sun disappears."

"Okay." The morning taunted her. She lay on her bed with a heavy feeling, as if someone were sitting on top of her.

"Are you packed?"

"Nope."

"Hurry up and do it," Sarah insisted. "We're leaving here in two hours. I want you all ready by no later than noon."

"Okay."

She staggered out of bed and wondered whether it would be quicker to dress or pack first. She pulled clothes out of the dresser and dumped them, like wash, in a suitcase. There was no time to sort anything. Unable to recall the combination for the lock, she pressed down on the snap and fastened the straps to shut the bag. She shoved her pocketbook, with her passport in the zipper compartment, under the mattress. Her bikini hung from a hook on the bathroom door, which she held open with one foot while she changed into the suit and brushed her teeth. That way she could watch out for someone trying to sneak into the cottage. She walked outside, pressing back a paranoiac urge to crouch and run zigzag, ducking an imagined bullet from Eddie's gun. The air was thick with heat. Clouds swirled over the sun, alternately veiling and revealing it. The sea, building to a light chop, provided a hint of wind.

With the holiday drawing to a close, Leslie felt her tan was fading and tried to refurbish it. A palm frond, like a louver, partially blocked the sun. Leslie raised herself slightly, maneuvering the chair under her body, to position herself directly in its rays. She oiled her body from top to bottom. A hand could slip on her skin or might pull away from the stickiness of the lotion. Oil slicks, she considered, reflected glints of sunlight, often creating a blinding target.

Concentrating on her tan relaxed Leslie and made her feel more confident. But it faded as fast as that mood. Her fidgeting on the chair caused the back of it to collapse with a bang. She jumped up, then rearranged herself sideways on the mat, with her knees pulled up and her head burrowed in them. She put on sunglasses to hide the troublesome thoughts pounding in her brain and creeping into her eyes like the onslaught of a migraine.

She rehearsed various stories she might tell Eddie. Multiple choices had always been the trouble with her life, and as usual she chose none of the above, now convinced that the headaches attacking with such frequency of late were the onset of a brain tumor—which, of course, would explain the casino episode. At such times, with powerful intimations of her own death, Leslie was filled with an urgency about living her life, a remission if not a reprieve.

It was time to go. Running into the sea, she flopped down

on a wave instead of easing into the water with a series of cold shocks that started at the knees and climaxed over the shoulders. Her strokes were rapid and firm, like those of a long-distance swimmer. She lifted her head out of the water for air and saw she was well past the buoy, a quarter-mile strand of outsized styrofoam pearls, and in shark territory just around the cove. The beach was a blur of miniature people and objects. Palm trees twisted in the wind. The increasing chop in the water made Leslie uneasy. She treaded water to steady herself. Anxious about her meeting with Eddie, was she imagining the undertow that seemed to drag her farther out? Leslie hoped for a mere sun shower, but felt the familiar patterns of a typical island squall. Surely Eddie would not be fool enough to drive the boat smack into it. There was no choice for her but to turn back, yet she could make no headway.

She heard the sputtering of a boat and quickened her pace to avoid its wake. A wave slapped her in the face. Her eyes stung. She tried to open them by picking apart the lashes stuck together with salt and suntan oil.

She blew her nose to restore her hearing, and now there was no confusion about the voice that spoke to Leslie from the boat. "Get in," Eddie commanded. The pain of that strong grip, hoisting her up, brought back her total terror. Without another word he drove the battered blue rowboat farther out, its outboard motor idling inside the folds of breaking waves. Suddenly the storm seemed to veer off.

"Did you talk to your daddy?" he asked sternly, waving her press card and the pink markers she had signed in her face.

"It's all fixed," Leslie said with a reassuring smile. She marveled at how, in a split second and without once having entertained the thought of resolving the matter this way, she had come up with the perfect solution. There was no time left for Eddie to check out the story and assuredly he would not want to rock the boat. Empowered with such ingenuity, she could not stop herself, elaborating to the point of unraveling her tale. "It's all set. My father has agreed to speak to your people's lawyers. He is very sympathetic and sure they could all work out a motion he can grant. It was amazingly simple. I never dreamed he would consider a thing like this seriously. I should have thought of doing it earlier. But I'll never forgive you for bullying me all over the place and wrecking my holiday."

Eddie picked at a cuticle on his thumbnail as if scraping away at her story. "It's all in writing, I take it," he mumbled, glancing sideways at her.

She felt her stomach sink and then, turning to ice, looked him straight in the eye and said, "Obviously you want to stay forever on this island or go to prison. You know perfectly well, Eddie, that number one, my father's not going to talk to you, and number two, he's not going to put anything in writing. So you are apparently determined to make a mess of everything you touch."

His light eyes turned steely. He lunged at Leslie.

Suddenly raindrops, the size of quarters, hammered them. Blackening clouds hurtled across the sky and swells climbed the sides of the boat, heaving water into it. The boat lurched and threw Eddie back in his seat. He twisted around to start the engine. A mammoth wave rose up like a black wall.

"Cut the engine or we'll go over," Leslie shrieked.

"I'll beat it."

The wave struck the boat, flipping it up and pitching them both overboard. For seconds that seemed an eternity, Leslie somersaulted helplessly. A wave shot her head above the surface. The water clogged her nose and mouth, almost gagging her. She spit up the sea.

Eddie, partially hidden by a huge swell, was gripping the gunwale. She swam toward him. Needles of rain slashed her. Lifting her head for air, she saw another gigantic wave wallop the boat, slamming it around. The motor struck Eddie's head.

Leslie broke into a rapid crawl, pounding the water with all her might. "Here," she yelled, "grab onto my hand." She heard a muffled cry, and Eddie's head, gushing blood, slipped below the surface.

She ducked underwater and grabbed him under his arms. She tried to hoist him over the rim of the boat, but he kept sliding back down into the water. She struggled to prop him up again.

An enormous wave pulled them apart. A frenzy propelled her, shooting power into her spent body. Leslie tried to beat back the waves to find him.

The squall was dying down to a mild choppiness on the sea. She paddled around the boat, circling it twice, calling out his name. Leslie heard only her own gasping breath, saw only a red stain on the water.

Nearby the markers were disintegrating in the sea.

Gone.

Exhausted, she knew she could not swim the whole distance and clambered back into the boat. She spotted a piece of soggy rope tied to an oarlock, untangled it and used it to crank up the engine. Numbness overcame her as she mechanically steered the boat. Plunging over the water, she stared coldly ahead at the beach and wondered if she had already missed her plane. At the buoy she ditched the boat and swam the rest of the way to shore.

Kicking the water out of her way, she stepped on the beach where her mother, hands on hips, now stood. "Where have you been?" she fumed. "I thought you had drowned. You'll miss the plane. Everyone else is ready. Shinehead took the bags to the airport earlier."

"I'm packed," Leslie moaned, hoping she did not look as stunned and bedraggled as she felt. Her legs were shaking, about to cave in, as she walked back to the cottage.

Inside the room she pulled off the bikini, letting it fall to the floor, and stepped into the shower. The water peeled off the salt and sand. Her tears merged with the spray of shower water. She dried herself hurriedly, slipped into pants and raced over the buttons of her blouse, missing and having to go back over them with trembling hands. She tugged the pocketbook out from under the mattress and fumbled for dark sunglasses to hide her eyes, red from salt sea and tears.

Everyone was piling into the cab as Leslie reached the driveway. It was noon, and a few tourists were coming off the tennis court to escape the blazing sun. Shinehead started up the car. They were on their way.

"Good-bye, Anlucia," Rebecca said in a dirge-like voice as she waved at the green hills, blue sea and native women toting straw baskets on their heads.

Shoving aside any sentimentality, their mother said, "Make sure the tourist cards are ready . . . the white ones you filled out when we arrived."

"Okay," Leslie mumbled, pretending to be lost in these instructions.

The judge, underlining legal papers, loaned his pen and continued to work with a stubby piece of pencil.

At the airport everyone said goodbye to Shinehead. A security officer whisked them through the luggage inspection area to the departure gate.

Leslie felt her mind slurring, fading in and out of interior conversation. "Get the money . . . *before* you leave . . . You won't get off the island alive." Eddie's clenched voice seemed to pinch her consciousness. A crowd of people shimmered in the sunlight bouncing off the tarmac, but all she saw was Eddie, his arms folded, a human barricade, stopping her at the departure gate and announcing coldly, "You come with me. . ."

Then came an announcement over the loudspeaker: "This is the final boarding call for British West Indian Airways Flight Nine Nine Seven, bound for the city of New York, John F. Kennedy Airport. Passengers please proceed through Gate Two and have their boarding passes ready."

"We have to go," her mother urged, poking Leslie. "Come on, right now."

Numbly, Leslie followed the family onto the airfield and climbed the stairs to the plane. Plopping down into a seat, she dropped her tennis rackets on the floor. Everyone was shoving carry-on luggage into overhead compartments. The hem of Rebecca's coat brushed the side of her face. Chilled, Leslie reached inside her tote bag, pulled out a beach towel and spread it over her lap. The flight attendant passed around menus and took drink orders. As the door of the plane whined shut, Rebecca squeezed past Leslie to get to her window seat. Then the plane, its engines roaring, rolled down the runway and lifted off into the blue horizon, unfolding a panorama of palm trees hugging the shoreline, green sea, and houses dotting the hills. The air was so still that it seemed, as the plane leveled off, that they were going nowhere. The sky always seemed to apologize after a squall. Leslie looked down at the tranquil water, wondering if anything moved there either. A tray table bumped her knee as the flight attendant unlatched it and set down a drink.

Leslie took a big swallow of scotch. As it went down, she felt a burning in her chest. She reached for the headset in the seat pocket to dilute her pain. The plane was climbing again, deserting the island and the horror she left there. Flicking the channels, she settled on hard rock and turned it up to the highest decibel. But the dissonance in her head flattened the music.

"Your arm is taking up too much room." Rebecca, seated beside her, nudged her elbow.

Leslie pretended to be asleep. As the plane glided into its final altitude, she faintly heard an announcement from her mother across the aisle.

"Children," she said, "I have reservations for next Christmas."